# ALEKSANDR

His Reluctant Submissive - Book One

## JESSIE JONES

Published by Blushing Books
An Imprint of
ABCD Graphics and Design, Inc.
A Virginia Corporation
977 Seminole Trail #233
Charlottesville, VA 22901

Jessie Jones
Aleksandr

eBook ISBN: 978-1-64563-892-6
Print ISBN: 978-1-64563-893-3
v1

T he man, dressed immaculately in the gray designer suit, sat in a private booth at the exclusive New York City restaurant sipping his glass of wine. A smile touched his full, pink lips as his silver-colored eyes slid over the bevy of beautiful women inspecting him as if he was their next meal. Maybe he would sample one of the tasty treats before making the long flight back to his home in Russia. After all, Aleksandr Volkov was not a man who denied himself the simple pleasures of life and frequently enjoyed the company of beautiful women. Although this visit was predominantly business, sex was always a nice way to release stress, and Aleksandr had more than his fair share of pressure. Not only was he the head of the largest bratva in his native homeland, but he was also trying to set up a legitimate business in the States. At this moment in time, there was a quiet, palpable tension building in the ranks of his organization. What complicated matters further, were the rumors of war being whispered amongst his men between his family and the second largest bratva in Russia. Aleksandr couldn't quite put his finger on the pulse of the problem but knew something big was about to go down. If there was one thing the mafia leader prided himself on, it was control of his vast empire, and he didn't play well with others who tried to fuck with that.

Hearing the soft sound of a woman clearing her throat brought Aleksandr out of his thoughts. His silver eyes slowly traveled up the form of an attractive, blonde woman standing before him in a tight, short skirt and white V-neck blouse. His gaze lingered on the large breasts spilling from the material before reaching out to touch her face. Aleksandr's voice was deep and masculine as he said, "Hello, little one. Is there something you need from me?"

The waitress giggled as her blue eyes slid over the large, strikingly handsome man. The man in front of her was gorgeous, clearly disgustingly rich, and there was an element of danger that made the foreign man even sexier. Hungrily licking her lips, she cooed, "I was wondering if I could get you anything to drink this evening. You can have anything you like, sir, even if it's not on the menu."

"I'll start with a Black Russian. We can discuss what else I would like after business." Aleksandr smiled affectionately, showing the waitress straight, white teeth. He then heard the breath catch in the waitress' voice when he eased his hand up the back of her thigh and under her short skirt to massage her bottom. Aleksandr licked his lips sensually and chuckled softly as he watched the young, attractive woman's knees begin to buckle when his finger traced the slit of her pussy through the bikini panties she wore. Done playing with her for the moment, Aleksandr removed his hand as his eyes touched hers. "I'll bring you pleasure later, sweetheart. Right now, bring my drink."

As the waitress scurried off quickly to do as Aleksandr instructed, he was unprepared to feel the hard grip on his left shoulder. Turning his head quickly, a smile touched his lips once again as he said, "'Bout fucking time, old man. I was beginning to think you had changed your mind."

"It looked like you just had your hands full, son. Somehow I doubt you were worried about me." Viktor Sergei laughed as he watched Aleksandr stand up before pulling the younger man into a loving embrace. Pulling back, he patted Aleksandr's bearded face affectionately. "To have a face like yours, my friend. Must be exhausting having so many women begging to be fucked."

Aleksandr chuckled before releasing Viktor and motioning for him to take a seat. As the two men sat down, he exhaled dramatically. "It can be quite taxing at times, but I seem to manage well. How have you been, old friend? You're looking rather tired. Is Anya keeping you up at night?"

"More than you know." Viktor laughed affectionately, thinking of his lovely wife. "Anya sends her love by the way and regrets that she can't join us, but she is not feeling well."

"I am sorry to hear that," Aleksandr replied, a concerned look on his face. Viktor was like a father to him and he cared deeply for the man who had taken him in as a child. "I hope it's nothing serious. Is there anything I can do for the two of you?"

"Actually, there is," Viktor quietly replied as he eyed the younger man intently. "You know I consider you and your brother to be my own children. God did not see fit to bless Anya and me with a son of our own, but he did bless us with you."

Aleksandr sat back and watched Viktor's body language stiffen and a sadness creep into the Russian elder's blue eyes. An icy chill shot up Aleksandr's spine; something was wrong and he knew it. "Get to the point, dammit. It's not like you to beat around the bush, Viktor."

With a loud sigh, the distinguished older man said, "No, it's not, so I will just say it, but this is strictly between the two of us and I will need your decision to my proposition before you leave this restaurant today. Understand?"

"I do," Aleksandr replied as he nodded his head in agreement. "Proceed."

Viktor let out a loud sigh as he raked an aging, wrinkled hand through his silver-streaked hair. "I'm dying," the older man blurted out as his eyes studied the younger man's face. "The doctors have told me that I have cancer and I only have six months to live. I knew I had been tired and not feeling well, but I did not anticipate this."

"Viktor…" Aleksandr began solemnly but was immediately silenced by the older man raising his hand.

"I don't need your pity or your sympathy, Alek," Viktor quickly said, knowing he could not stand to hear the younger man's words, for fear he would break down in front of him. "But I do need your help. Anya is not here today because she still has not come to terms with my diagnosis. This meeting is not intended for mourning, my son, but rather a business proposition. When I'm gone, I will need you to take care of my wife and daughters, both physically and monetarily. Will you do that for me?"

"Of course, Viktor," Aleksandr replied, stunned by the man's words. He could not believe the man before him, who looked like a pillar of muscle and strength, was dying of cancer. Death, clearly, was the great equalizer. "You can rest knowing that they will always be taken care of, but you knew that already, old friend. What is it that you are really wanting from me? I sense your hesitation, and it makes me uneasy. Just spit it out already."

"Fine," the older man replied with a growl as he pounded a fist on the table. Leave it to the younger man to read between the lines and see the truth hidden underneath. If there was one thing Aleksandr Volkov was good at, it was reading people, and that was why Viktor was about to ask him for the biggest favor of his life. "Upon my death, Alek, you will take over as head of my bratva."

"No," the man with dirty-blond hair growled through clenched, white teeth. He had anticipated that this was coming, and quite frankly, he didn't want it. Not only was Viktor the leader of the third largest bratva, but he had just inked a multi-billion-dollar deal to expand his business to the States. In recent months, there had been so much turmoil within Viktor's mafia family that he had enlisted Aleksandr's help to clean things up. The elderly man was brilliant but lacked tight control over what belonged to him. Aleksandr was not a fan of drugs or forced prostitution, and both were rampant there. It would take months, or even years, to weed out the bad seeds, and he lived by a sort of honor among thieves' code. Aleksandr might be a killer, but there was a fairness to his method of madness.

"Yes!" Viktor shouted as he stood up and banged his fist on the table. Switching to their native tongue, he said, "I have already met with the members of the council and set the plan into action. You will be my successor whether you like it or not!"

"Fuck you, old man!" Aleksandr yelled back as he shot to his feet. The entire restaurant turned at his deep, elevated, masculine voice. "I decide my fate, not you! I told you I don't fucking want it, and last I checked, you had no problems with your hearing!"

"You have to do this for me, Alek!" Viktor pleaded through clenched teeth as he lowered his voice so the people around them would stop staring. "Think of the money that will be at your disposal. My empire is worth more than half a billion dollars. All of that will belong to you; just say the word."

A harsh, derisive laugh escaped Aleksandr's lips as his eyes darkened dangerously to a steel-grey hue. "Half a billion dollars! Are you forgetting that I am one of the wealthiest men in the world? My net worth exceeds twelve billion. Your empire would be pocket change for me. You know why I don't want it, Viktor. I love you like a father and I respect you greatly, but your control of your bratva has been slipping for some time. I don't have time to clean up your fucking mess!"

Before Viktor could respond, he suddenly fell back in his chair as a wave of dizziness swept through him and a sudden, intense pain shot across his temple. When he felt Aleksandr's large hands gripping his shoulders in concern, Viktor jerked away and broke the younger man's grip. "Don't!" he barked, raising his hands. "Just give me a minute, dammit! It'll pass."

Aleksandr gritted his teeth as he released the older man but continued to stand over him with a concerned, protective stance. *Damn, Viktor,* he thought to himself! He was feeling an immense guilt for yelling at the bastard but felt an even greater pain in his chest at the news of his terminal condition. Aleksandr had no idea the man was even sick, let alone dying. Viktor knew he would never have considered being his successor, so the older man was using his current position to try to manipulate Aleksandr into somehow feeling sorry for him, and dammit, it was beginning to work!

---

Viktor sat with his eyes closed as the pain in his head began to subside. Tears brimmed behind his closed eyelids. The last person he wanted to see him weak like this was the younger man he considered a son. "Alek," Viktor began, his voice soft and full of emotion. "I know the control of my territories has decreased in the last two to three years, but I have been so focused on the shit Paul has been scheming that I have become somewhat obsessed with him, unfortunately at the cost of losing solid ground in the underworld."

Aleksandr ran an exasperated hand through his dishwater

blond hair at the mention of Paul Morrison. The American bastard had married Viktor's daughter Kira two years ago and was a cowardly weasel whom Aleksandr absolutely hated. Paul was an international businessman who had several politicians in his back pocket and knew how to skirt the law. The asshole was making a mockery of Viktor's leadership or what it meant to be in a bratva and was allowing things into the Russian mafia that they had weeded out years ago. Paul had also started a bad habit of asserting himself as Viktor's second in command, and it was pissing off several members of the council. Not only was Paul bad for business, but everyone knew he was sleeping with multiple women and abusive to Kira. She, of course, denied the abuse and blindly followed where Paul led.

"I know you are angry with me, probably feeling manipulated, and I'm sorry for that," Viktor said, interrupting Aleksandr's thoughts. "I knew what your reaction would be, though. I was hoping you would take charge long enough to straighten things out or give leadership to someone you trusted, like your brother Nikolai. My pride won't allow me to beg you..."

At that moment, a building of a man walked up to the table and bent down to whisper something into Viktor's ear. When the large, Russian guard walked away, Viktor looked at Aleksandr as he stood up and began buttoning his suit jacket. "I'm sorry to do this, but I have to go. Apparently, my daughter Kira is in some sort of trouble that needs my attention immediately. Since you clearly need time to think about my proposition, I will give you until tomorrow evening to give me an answer. I should warn you that even if you say no, my council will seek you out upon my death. Like it or not, things have already been set into motion."

Before turning to leave, Viktor looked into Aleksandr's darkened eyes and felt an icy chill race up his spine. The younger man was clearly enraged, and he hated to admit it, but Viktor feared Aleksandr, even though the two were close. Although his words said otherwise, Viktor knew Aleksandr would do what he wanted. He only hoped that Aleksandr's love for him trumped the anger he felt. If Viktor wasn't dying, he knew there was no way he could have gotten away with talking to Alek the way he had. Breaking eye contact with the silver-eyed man, Viktor turned to leave. He heard the loud gasps of surprise as he simultaneously heard the crashing of the table and dishes. Viktor had left just in time.

---

"Fuck!" Aleksandr yelled as he flipped the table. His large body was tense with rage as he picked up a heavy chair and threw it across the room. Viktor had better be glad he was sick and that Aleksandr loved him like a father, because those were the only things saving his sorry ass right now. As his eyes shot around the room at the many patrons staring in stunned silence, Aleksandr watched men and women alike turn their heads away from him in total fear. No one wanted to feel his wrath. He might be extremely wealthy and have the face of an angel, but even the devil feared the lethal and merciless Aleksandr Volkov.

Needing to release some of his anger and frustration before he killed the next man who stepped in his path, Aleksandr motioned to his most trusted guard and quickly made his way out of the restaurant. Thirty minutes later, he found himself walking into the discreet sex club designed for the wealthy and elite. On the surface, Nona was a small nightclub, but to those in the know, it was a place where one's deepest, darkest fantasies were fulfilled, and right now, Aleksandr needed a distraction from his rage. Just as he stepped up to the bar to get a glass of vodka, he turned his head and was stunned to see the pale-skinned redhead rapidly making her way toward the back of the club. The woman was built like an hourglass and dressed in a tight, black, slip dress that emphasized every delicious inch of her body. The black material hugged her smaller frame and emphasized her wide hips and lovely breasts, which made his cock begin to pulse with anticipation. Aleksandr couldn't see the woman's face but knew she would be amazing to look at. A smile touched his pink lips at the thought of wrapping those shapely, slender legs around his waist as he fucked her intensely. With that thought, Aleksandr watched her talk to a blonde woman before exiting through a set of double doors. The only reason the red-haired beauty would disappear through the doors was if she were looking for some fun, and Aleksandr would be more than happy to help her with that.

Needing to see the woman's face, Aleksandr downed the drink before he shot across the club. He could feel an electric current growing in the base of his spine as he made his way into the back of the building. Looking around, he growled and let out an explicative when the woman was nowhere to be seen. Where the fuck could she have gone? Was she a submissive? Did she belong to the owner? Aleksandr had so many questions racing through his mind that he did not see the ebony-haired woman approach him from behind.

"Mr. Volkov?" she asked, almost whisper soft as he turned to glare at her. Seeing the irritation in his silver eyes, she quickly offered, "I'm sorry if I startled you, but I thought you looked lost. Can I help you with something this evening?"

"Da. Did you see a redhead in a tight, black dress walk through here?"

"Of course. She has an appointment with Master Andrei. Do you know her?"

Ignoring the woman's question, Aleksandr asked, "Where is Andrei this evening? I need to speak to him right away."

"Come. I'll take you to him."

Aleksandr followed the scantily clad woman as she led him toward the owner of the club and one of his best friends. The two had grown up together before Andrei had moved to the States with his parents in his late teens. They had moved his friend and changed his name, to keep a rival bratva from killing him. Now he owned several sex clubs in the States that catered to the wealthy and elite. Andrei didn't know it, but Aleksandr had kept an eye on his friend the entire time and had guards who watched him 24/7.

Walking into Andrei's office, Aleksandr was not surprised to see him sitting on the edge of his desk, talking on the phone. If there was one thing Andrei liked to do, it was talk. As he hung up the phone, his blue eyes found Aleksandr as he yelled loudly, "Alek, you crazy son of a bitch! Why didn't you call me and let me know you were in town?"

The two men hugged and laughed as Aleksandr smiled. "I was not anticipating finding pleasure while here, my friend, but it has appeared to find me."

"Is that so? Well, you are always welcome to my submissives. Your brother, Nikolai, was just here a couple days ago. That one is quite a hit with my loves. It must be that pretty face of his. Now, what can I do for you? I hate to rush you, brat, but I have an appointment that I am late for."

"Your appointment is exactly what I would like to talk to you about, Andrei." Aleksandr smiled as he watched his friend step back and cross his arms over his large chest in irritation. "I saw a young woman with an amazing body and red hair who, I was told, was your next appointment. Is that true? If so, I want her."

Andrei began to shake his head vigorously as he shouted in their native language, "No fucking way, Alek. This is one woman I refuse to share." At Aleksandr's arched, golden brow, he said, "Besides, she's specific with what she likes. She is not going to let just any man crawl on top of her. It has taken me a year or more to develop our relationship. I'm not going to let you fuck that up."

"Need I remind you, Andrei, that I'm not just any man. There isn't a woman alive who has ever refused me. I doubt she will be the first." Aleksandr smiled, intrigued by Andrei's quick refusal. He had never seen the Dom react this way to a woman, even his most treasured submissive, Elena. What about the redhead was so special? Walking over to the wall parallel to where Andrei sat on the desk, Aleksandr hit a hidden button and stood back as a panel slid slowly and revealed an elegant, masculine bedroom. As his eyes touched the two-way mirror, the breath caught in his throat as his cock slammed against the zipper of his pants.

Before Aleksandr, stood the most ravishing creature he had ever had the pleasure of looking at. The woman was even more beautiful up close than she had been from a distance. Nothing, though, could have prepared Aleksandr for the jolt of lust and need that shot through his body as he stared at the alluring enchantress. He not only wanted her sexually but wanted to possess every inch of her. Never in his thirty-eight years of existence, had Aleksandr been this attracted to a woman. He could not pull his eyes from her as she began to take off her clothes, let alone hear his friend Andrei speaking to him. Aleksandr watched her pull the black slip dress she wore over her mid-back, her magenta-red hair framing a lovely face, with eyes that appeared violet in color. She chewed on her full, wide lip and scrunched her pert, well-formed nose as she smoothed her hair down in the mirror. As his eyes traveled down her body, Aleksandr could not stop the moan that escaped his lips. Round, close set breasts were decorated with protruding, light-pink nipples and a well-manicured, triangle of bright red hair met him as his eyes went even lower. He then watched her turn on shapely, well-toned legs and carry her small, narrow waist and perfect alabaster ass to Andrei's bed before crawling in and pulling the sheet up over her body. Her skin was flawless and porcelain and looked as soft as white lilies. Aleksandr found his mouth watering as he pictured his face buried in that succulent pussy as she wiggled beneath him, begging him to let her come. Fuck, he needed to be inside this woman, and he needed it now!

"Oh shit," Andrei moaned when Aleksandr finally pulled his eyes from the woman and found him. He could see the look on his friend's face and knew that his time with his favorite client would be abruptly coming to an end. "Look, man, you have to promise me that you will treat El with the utmost respect. She is not like other women."

"Does she belong to you? Is she your submissive?" Aleksandr asked, his silver eyes narrowing on his friend as he gripped Andrei's shirt and jerked him forward. "How long have you been fucking her?"

"No, she doesn't belong to me. What the hell is wrong with you? Let go of me!" Andrei yelled back, just as Aleksandr loosened his grip and shoved the Russian Dom back. Catching his breath, Andrei looked at his best friend, who stood like a towered, brick wall with his arms over his broad chest waiting for an answer. "Stop looking at me like that, dammit! She's not my submissive, and I technically am not fucking her!"

"What do you mean you're not technically fucking her? Why is she naked in your bed then?"

"I already told you Alek, El isn't typical," Andrei replied, needing a stiff drink. As he walked over to his mini bar to pour himself one, he said, "Look, I'm not sleeping with her like you think. El has been coming here for about six months, and I only eat her pussy and use toys occasionally. She won't let me go any further, although I have definitely tried, believe me. I don't know if she's married or in a relationship. Fuck! I don't even know her real name. All I know is she has a professional career, and she has asked me to call her El. She comes in when she needs a release. If you want a shot at her, then go ahead and try! I'm telling you, though, Alek, she will shoot you down without batting an eye. El has spunk."

Aleksandr walked up to Andrei, took the drink from his hand and downed it. He then patted his friend on the cheek affectionately as a brilliant smile touched his lips. "We'll see about that. Now if you'll excuse me, I don't want to keep our guest waiting." Aleksandr then released Andrei and turned to leave the room.

# Chapter 2

Sophia Rousseau sat on the bed waiting for Andrei to enter the room. She brushed her hair back over her shoulder and considered leaving. She had so much damn work to do, but that was part of the reason she was visiting Andrei's club. As one of the world's top international attorneys, Sophia had stacks of files in her downtown office requiring her attention, but she needed something to help her relax and refocus. The latter thought was exactly why she sat naked in Andrei's bed. She had no time for a traditional relationship due to her work schedule, but luckily for her, she had heard her secretary talking about the dominant and the types of services he offered. Sophia had a big day in court tomorrow and just needed to unwind a little. Maybe tonight, she would let Andrei go further than he had in the past six months. She needed to be fucked good and hard, but there was something about him that made her put on the brakes. Andrei was handsome, foreign and dominant, but he lacked something that Sophia could not quite understand. *I'll just stick to some oral*, she thought to herself as she heard the door to the room open.

The air was sucked from Sophia's lungs when she saw a

mountain of a man step into the room, only to stand in the doorway and stare at her. Her mouth dropped open as she sat and gawked at what had to be the most gorgeous man in the world. He was dressed in a designer suit, stood about six-foot-six, and was a solid wall of hard, lean muscle, with deeply tanned, tattooed skin. What appeared to be eyes the color of a shiny, metallic gray, bored into Sophia, and her pussy immediately began to throb with anticipation. The hair on his head was a dirty-blond color and cut fashionably short, with the edges buzzed and the top fuller and spiky. His face was masculine and rugged, with a thin, straight nose and a well-manicured, Hollywoodian style beard that matched his hair and was tinged with gray. Sophia watched a slow, sensual smile spread across his full, wide lips as his eyes focused on her bare breasts. She could tell by the glint in his eyes that this man was dangerous, sexual and arrogant as hell. Damn, this man was the most tantalizing piece of masculinity Sophia had ever laid eyes on. Her entire being was drawn to him, and that scared her. What the hell was wrong with her? This man was a stranger! Where the hell was Andrei?

When Sophia noticed the stranger begin to remove his suit jacket and lay it on the end of the bed, she suddenly found her voice. "Don't come any closer! Who the hell are you, and where is Andrei?"

"Name is Alek. Andrei is busy," Aleksandr offered, wanting to ease the fear he saw leap into her violet eyes. Fuck, this woman was breathtaking up close! "He sent me to please you."

"No, I don't believe you," Sophia countered suspiciously. "Andrei didn't say anything to me about introducing someone else into our sessions. I want to see him."

"I told you. Andrei is busy. I'll give you pleasure this evening," Aleksandr replied casually as he began to unbutton the cuffs of his long-sleeved shirt.

Sophia inhaled a deep, shaky breath as her eyes watched

him begin to manipulate the buttons on his linen shirt. She hungrily licked her lips when it opened and he revealed a massive, broad chest covered with light blond hair and ornate tattoos. She could feel her insides melting at the sight of his exquisite body. Sophia hated to admit it, but she would let this man do any damn thing he wanted to her! Shaking herself mentally, Sophia jerked her eyes up to his face and was pissed to see a superior, haughty smile on his face. His eyes told her that he knew how much she wanted him, and that infuriated her even more. "Stop taking your clothes off, dammit, and get out! I want to see Andrei right now!"

Seeing that she was getting even more upset, Aleksandr stopped his movements and motioned to the end of the bed. "May I sit?" When she hesitantly nodded her head, Aleksandr took a seat on the California king bed. Looking directly into her eyes, he smiled. "Let me ease your mind, sweet one, and cut to the chase. I want to fuck you, not hurt you. I saw you enter the club this evening, and I followed you back here. Andrei told me that you were here to see him, but I told him I would take you off his hands. Do I look like I need to hurt women to sleep with them?"

"No, you don't, but neither did Ted Bundy," Sophia countered sarcastically as his eyes narrowed at her. There was something about the way he spoke and the sincerity Sophia saw briefly flash in his eyes, that told her she could trust him. Sophia loved an aggressive man, and he clearly was just that. She felt her heart begin to race and leap into her throat when he mentioned intentionally seeking her out. God help her, but she wanted him too. *You must be losing your damn mind*, she shouted at herself. "Look, just because you're an attractive man doesn't mean you're not dangerous. If you're friends with Andrei, why haven't I seen you here before?"

"I am visiting from my homeland Russia. I saw you walk in tonight and had to find out who you were. I have pleased many of his submissives over the years, but none as beautiful as you. I was hoping to do the same for you," Alek replied as the pulse in his jaw began to tick. Damn, this woman was feisty! She should be falling at his feet instead of sitting here questioning him. "If you don't belong to Andrei, then who owns you?"

Sophia made a scoffing noise before she chuckled softly and rolled her violet eyes. "No one owns me. I see Andrei because I need a release every now and then. The women in your country may be owned, but here, we do as we please. I don't have to explain my actions to you or anyone."

With a growl of frustration, Alek reached across the bed and grabbed Sophia in one swift motion. Hauling her voluptuous, struggling, naked body across his lap, he brought her face inches from his to say in a low, husky voice, "Oh, I think you do. For the next couple hours, I own every inch of this delicious body. You can lie and say you don't want me, but your body tells me otherwise. What is your safe word?"

Sophia could feel his warm, minty breath against her lips as he spoke. She also could smell his intoxicating, masculine, and savory scent and felt her nipples harden into sharp, pointy nubs. God, she wanted this man more than she had ever wanted anyone before! Sophia could see herself seeking this man out for more than just sex. Good thing she didn't let people get too close, because she could see Alek doing just that. Did she let this man have his way with her, or did she leave? Before she knew it, she heard herself ordering softly, "Pigeon. My safe word is pigeon. You only do what Andrei would do, and you keep your pants on."

"For now, I will keep my pants on, but let's get one thing straight. I don't take orders from you, but you will obey mine." Alek smiled, his large, hardened cock rubbing painfully against the zipper of his slacks. He inhaled her sweet, flowery scent as his nose traveled up her neck and the side of her porcelain face. When his mouth found hers, he ran his tongue along her rose-colored lips and began massaging one large, bare breast.

Pulling back her head abruptly, Sophia gasped loudly. "I don't kiss. It's too personal."

"Oh, but I do, and so will you," Alek replied simply, before he slammed his mouth against hers in a demanding, passionate kiss. Feeling her pushing against his chest, he deepened the kiss and quickly had her straddling his thick thighs. In one spontaneous, rapid motion, Alek had Sophia on her back in the center of the bed and her hands locked above her head. Rubbing his giant, clothed cock against her core, he felt her legs instinctually wrapping around his waist and her undulating her pussy against his zipper. He also felt Sophia melting into his kiss before she, too, brought her tongue into play with his. Breaking the kiss, Alek trailed a path of kisses up to her ear. "Good girl. You learn quickly. I like that. Now I am going to explore your body. You know what to do if you want me to stop."

Sophia was breathless as she nodded her head quickly before his lips connected with hers again in a softer, more lighthearted kiss. When he sat back on his ankles between her legs, Sophia felt the warm, salty liquid dripping from her core. This man was delicious to look at and made every single inch of her body tingle with sensation. Sophia's porcelain skin blushed bright pink as his silver eyes slowly scanned every inch of her. Her clit began to pulse when his eyes locked on her core and two of his fingers found the hard, achy nub before sliding deeper inside. Her lavender eyes then watched the Russian giant pull out his fingers before sliding them into his mouth to suck off the juices.

Aleksander closed his eyes a moment as he sucked her sweet, delectable taste off his fingers. Fuck, she tasted like heaven! The woman's body was exquisite and so tiny compared to his large size. He loved the way the blush carried across her alabaster skin and the way her eyes scoured his body hungrily. The sensations coursing through his body were electric and unlike anything he had ever felt before. Since seeing the redhead across Andrei's club, he had forgotten all about his troubles with Viktor and the shit he was going to have to clean up. Maybe his trip to America was going to be better than he had anticipated.

Sophia moaned in pure pleasure when he pressed down her inner thighs to open her legs wide before he bent his blond head to run his tongue around one nipple. When he looked up her body, her eyes locked with his as he playfully nibbled on the bud before he sucked it into his mouth. At the same time, Aleksandr's large, rough hands massaged her inner thighs. Sophia's body jerked and her back arched in ecstasy when she felt one hand begin to slowly massage her clit. She heard him chuckle deeply and watched him trail a path of kisses down her flat stomach to her well-manicured mound. Her hands gripped the sheets on the bed when she felt his hot breath hovering above the slick, moist folds. Aleksandr's slow, amazing movements had her pussy weeping and were driving her mad with anticipation.

Placing a chaste kiss on the mound of her cunt, Aleksandr's silver eyes again met hers. He moved two fingers leisurely in and out of her dripping, wet pussy as a smile touched his lips. "Do you want me to stop?" When she let out a shaky breath and shook her head no, Alek said huskily, "I need to hear the words, El. I will leave you lying here on the bed alone unless I hear you speak. So, what will it be?"

Sophia's head fell back a moment in pleasure as Aleksandr quickened the pace with his fingers. Just as abruptly, her head shot up when he stopped his movements and removed his fingers. She grabbed his wrist in both of her hands as she hurriedly and breathlessly whispered, "Please... don't... stop. Please..."

Aleksandr let out a deep, masculine chuckle before he placed a chaste kiss on her lips. He then placed a kiss on each of her nipples. Looking deep into her eyes as his mouth hovered above hers, Aleksandr slid his two, long fingers back into her cunt as he said in a husky, intense tone, "Good pet. Now tell Master Alek to lick your pussy."

Resisting the urge to bury her tongue in his mouth in a passionate kiss, Sophia heard herself purr, "Lick my pussy, Sir."

Alek ran his tongue along her bottom lip before he lowered himself between her legs and spread her vaginal lips wide with his free hand. A slow, sexy grin spread across his mouth when he saw the clear liquid pulsing from her core and pooling on the sheets under her bottom. Damn, he had never seen a pussy so wet before, and he couldn't wait to devour it. Denying himself the pleasure no longer, Alek slowly and methodically ran his tongue up her folds before he began sucking on the hooded clit. He heard what sounded like a loud purr escape her mouth before her hand gripped his dirty-blond hair and pushed his face closer to her warmth.

---

Sophia thrashed wildly on the bed and undulated against Aleksandr's mouth as he pleasured her body. Time and time again, he brought her to the brink of an orgasm, only to slow his rhythm and run kisses up and down the insides of her thighs. Her attraction to the man between her legs was unlike any she had ever felt before. Sophia could not believe the sensations coursing through her body or how much she wanted to feel all of him deep inside her. The feel of his mouth on her core had her panting and begging him not to stop. Feeling his movements slowing again, she sat up, propped on her elbows and looked down between her thighs. A blush covered her body and erupted into flames when she saw him resting his chin on her well-manicured mound as he looked into her eyes.

"Do you like the way my tongue feels, pet?" Alek asked casually, rubbing his bearded face against the velvety, red fuzz.

"Y-yes," Sophia stammered, her eyes searching his. This man was driving her insane with his actions!

"Yes, what?" Alek asked, cocking one golden brow at her.

"Yes, Sir. I like the way your mouth feels."

"Would you like to come in my mouth, pet?"

"Yes, Sir."

"Then ask me nicely," Aleksandr commanded as he leisurely circled one nipple with his free hand while he picked up the pace of the fingers moving in and out of her cunt.

With a loud moan of pure, unadulterated pleasure, Sophia fell back on the bed and said in an anguished cry, "Sir, may I come in your mouth?"

"Yes, pet," The Russian directed before his wet, hot tongue again engulfed her clitoris.

Sophia was unprepared for the scream that left her lips as the orgasm tore through her small, porcelain frame. She felt the room spinning and her vision begin to blacken before she closed her lavender eyes and rode the intensity of the wave. Her clit pulsed and throbbed in his mouth as Aleksandr sucked every drop of her sweet, salty essence from her pussy. Her hips bucked uncontrollably against his face and she couldn't help the agonized cries of pleasure from deep within. As the intense pressure began to subside, she felt the gorgeous giant placing a path of kisses up her thighs, stomach, breasts, and neck. When his mouth reached hers, Sophia's hands slid around his thick, corded neck and into his hair, so she could deepen the kiss.

Breaking the kiss as he rubbed his clothed, enlarged cock against her, Aleksandr still felt heady himself from the taste of her. "You tasted amazing, pet, like sweet, warm honey. I've never tasted anything like it before." Aleksandr then raised himself up to sit back on his heels as he began to unbuckle his pants. He reached into his pants to pull out his thick, enormous dick. As precum oozed from its mushroom-shaped head, he asked huskily, "Now that I've had the pleasure of tasting yours, would you like to taste mine?"

Sophia hungrily licked her lips as she nodded her head yes. Her eyes immediately dropped to his massive cock and her hand shot out to grip it. Her petite, porcelain fingers could not completely encircle his girth due to its size, so she began to massage the veiny underside. Her mouth watered at the thought of sucking on the large, delicious treat. She didn't even know how she was going to be able to get her mouth around it, but she sure would try. There was nothing little about Alek, and she found herself loving every inch of his body. Needing to please him as he had her, Sophia positioned herself on all fours in front of him in the center of the bed.

---

Alek smiled down at his sexy, obedient spitfire who was looking up at him with wide, lavender eyes. Fuck, she was magnificent! He couldn't wait to feel her mouth and pussy wrapped around his cock. She had hidden nothing from him, and he had literally lost his breath at how beautiful she had looked when she came for him. Sliding his hand over the hand on his cock, Alek helped her stroke him as he brought the tip of it to her lips. Just as he pushed his way in between her lips, the door to the room burst open.

"Get the fuck out!" Alek growled loudly as Sophia's small tongue circled the head of his dick.

"I'm sorry to interrupt, Aleksandr, but Viktor is dead," Andrei blurted out in Russian as his friend looked at him in disbelief.

"Fuck!" Aleksandr yelled as he quickly got off the bed and began picking up his clothes from the floor. As he threw on his shirt and began to button it, he sat down on the bed beside a very confused and dazed El. "Look at me, sweet one." When she did, he loosely gripped her chin in his scarred hand. "I'm sorry to end this so abruptly, but there is an emergency and I have to leave. I'm not done with you, though. I want you back here, tomorrow night, naked in this bed, at ten thirty exactly. Do I make myself clear?"

Trying to shake herself out of what felt like a fog, Sophia whispered softly, "Yes, I understand. I'll be here."

Aleksandr then searched her eyes a moment before his lips found hers for a hard, passionate kiss. Just as he felt her body begin to melt into his once again, Aleksandr let out a loud string of profanity before he abruptly stood up and stalked toward the door. Before he exited the room, he turned and took one more look at Sophia before leaving.

## Chapter 3

The beautiful, violet-eyed woman shot up in the bed as she heard the melodic ringing. Picking up the phone from the bedside table, Sophia cursed loudly as she glanced at the number lighting up the screen. What in the hell could Hallsey possibly want at one in the morning? Letting out a loud sigh of annoyance, she knew this couldn't be good. A phone call at this time of morning from one of her associates never was.

"Hello," the woman softly said as she put the cool metal to her ear. After listening for a minute, she quickly said, "Give me an hour, and I will meet you at the downtown office."

Clicking off the phone, Sophia tossed the small, electronic gadget to the side before she collapsed back on the bed. What in the hell was going on tonight? Sophia had finally just gotten into her own bed after her encounter with the Russian Dom at Andrei's club. Her entire body was still humming from his touch and she could still smell him all over her skin. Sophia also could not get over how she had acted like a wanton hussy with Alek and how easily he had made her beg for his touch. The giant had made her feel sensations she had never felt before, and that scared the hell out of her. Pushing all thoughts of the man out of her head, Sophia quickly hopped off the bed and made her way into the bathroom. After she washed up, she then pulled her vibrant, red hair into a pony-tail. When she was finished, she dashed into her walk-in closet where she slid a pair of stylishly torn blue jeans over her wide hips before throwing on an old, black concert t-shirt. After donning a pair of tennis shoes, the violet-eyed beauty grabbed her phone and briefcase before heading out of her penthouse suite and into the elevator. When she entered the downstairs lobby, Sophia found an elderly man holding the door for her.

"Leaving for work at this hour, Ms. Rousseau?" the doorman asked with a wide smile and admiring eyes as they traveled over her simple attire. "I thought you told me you were taking a couple days off."

"I was, Clarence, but duty calls, unfortunately." Sophia smiled back, exiting the building. "Could you be a dear and get me a car?"

Five minutes later, Sophia was climbing into the back of the sleek, silver sedan. She stifled a yawn as she laid her head back against the seat and closed her eyes. *Maybe I can just sleep on the way to the office*, she thought as the driver made his way through the busy streets of New York. However, even as that precious notion entered her mind, it was quickly replaced with a hundred questions and all of them centered on the phone call from Hallsey. She had never heard that tone in her friend's voice before. The two had been partners in a law firm for the last five years, and Sophia had never heard uncertainty or worry before tonight. The easy-going Englishman had an urgency in his voice that had made the hair stand up on the back of her neck. So much for the small vacation she had planned on taking this week. Her private beach cottage would just have to wait.

Her eyes closed once again, as her thoughts drifted to the

craziness that was her life. At thirty-two years of age, she had done quite well for herself. Sophia was not only a successful criminal attorney who dealt in international affairs, but was also a partner in one of the most prestigious law firms in the world. Not too bad for a gal who was born in the Parisian slums of France to a French drug lord living his life on the run with his barely legal American wife. Sophia had made her way to the states at the age of eleven, when her mother and father had been gunned down in the streets. She had lived with her older brother, Adam, for two years before he, too, had been killed. Sophia had then been brought to America by her mother's brother, Aaron, and raised by her grandmother. Her grandmother had been a very loving woman who had ensured that Sophia had been given the best education, although she barely had two pennies to rub together. She had not only graduated high school two years early, but she had also graduated with top honors from Yale Law School at the age of twenty-three. Her grandmother, Ava, had lived to see her graduate college but had passed away two weeks later of cancer. After quickly scurrying up the corporate ladder, Sophia had become the youngest woman ever to make partner with the firm of Abrams and Hall, now Abrams, Hall, and Rousseau.

Although Sophia had been blessed with great success in her professional life, she could not say the same thing about her personal life. As busy as her career kept her, the alabaster-skinned woman's love life was practically nonexistent. Sophia had no time for relationships or dating and had only found time for casual sex with a couple of partners. Plus, there was also the little fact that she was cursed when it came to men. Not only had she lost her father and brother to violence, but her first real boyfriend had died the same way. After he had died, Sophia had sworn off getting involved with men in anything other than a casual or friendly relationship. Her lack of companionship wasn't because she couldn't get a man, quite the opposite, really. Truth be told, Sophia wished at times that she wasn't quite so attractive. Men treated her like an object and assumed she was just another pretty face. She found most men weak, pathetic, and boring. Deep down, Sophia wanted a man who was dominant, strong, and masculine. The red-haired woman had grown up watching movies about handsome men sweeping their mates off their feet. How she wished fate would send her someone like that, but she would probably be too busy to even notice him. Even if she did, Sophia would sleep better at night knowing that he was safe, and she was alone.

Growing up in the Parisian slums, had been hard. She had spent most of her time with her mother, because her father was frequently away on 'business'. When he was home, he doted on her and was very affectionate. Her mother, although loving, was too young and inexperienced when it came to taking care of a child. Sophia's father had been involved deeply in the illegal drug trade but never brought it home. He not only dealt drugs in France, but around the world. As far as Sophia knew, her father had no family except those he trusted in the underworld. She had loved him deeply, despite the lifestyle he led. She had grown up around a lot of men but had never known how despicable or corrupt most of them were until she became an attorney. Sophia's father had died because of involvement in crime, and his death had propelled her toward a career in law.

With a loud sigh, she couldn't help but think of Alek as she thought about her father. Sophia's father had always been a large man who oozed danger and darkness from every pore. Although most had feared him, he had been so loving and affectionate with her. Alek oozed the same dangerous and deadly energy and was probably a criminal of some sort, but damn, how gorgeous he was to look at! She had been drawn to Alek like a moth to a flame and had instantly been attracted to the intensity of emotions pouring from his body. She had wanted that man the moment he walked into the room and was glad that their time together had been abruptly interrupted. Sophia wasn't sure what had occurred, but she could tell by Alek's response that it wasn't good. She had left Club Nona immediately after her giant had gone and had absolutely no intention of meeting him again. The man made her feel too much, and Sophia didn't like that at all.

Feeling the car come to a stop, her eyes flew open. Stretching out her body, she hadn't even realized that she had briefly dozed off. When the door to the sedan opened, she quickly made her way inside the high-end office and up to the top floor. Flying into the boardroom, Sophia was not surprised to see Hallsey sitting at the head of the long table, with files spread out before him. Hallsey, aka Cristofer Hall, looked stressed out, and if the bottle of whiskey sitting beside him was any indication, Sophia was in for a long night.

"Louie! I'm so damn glad to see you!" Hallsey said, referring to Sophia by the name that most men in the business called her. She had earned the nickname in college, when a first-year law professor had told her she should have been born a man because she was much too fierce to be a woman. Her middle name also happened to be Elouise.

"Cris, what in the hell is going on?" she asked, walking into the room and taking a seat.

"The proverbial shit has hit the fan, babe," Hallsey replied, shaking his head before putting the bottle of whiskey to his lips to take a long drink. Putting the bottle down on the table, his eyes found hers and he bluntly said, "Viktor Sergei is dead."

"What? How did he die?" Sophia yelled in surprise. She had personally met Viktor and his wife at a party and found the man to be very likable. He was a prominent Russian diplomat and worth a fortune.

"He was murdered a few hours ago, stabbed to death outside the gates of his home. Not only did they kill him, but they killed his daughter Kira as well," Hallsey replied as his hand tiredly ran over his bearded face. "They apparently have a suspect in custody, and the guy is making bail as we speak."

Sophia leaned back in her chair in stunned silence. She could not believe that someone had killed a man like Viktor. He was a kind soul who would give anyone the shirt off his back. He had done so much good in the last few years, and Sophia had a hard time understanding why someone would murder him so brutally. "So, you're telling me they caught the perp already? How did the guy make bail without representation? Wait a minute, Hallsey, I'm lost. As sad as I am to hear that Viktor and his daughter were murdered, how exactly does this involve us?"

"The perp is our, or should I say your, new case, Louie," Hallsey said as he slid a file her way.

Sophia rolled her eyes at Hallsey's words. Roman Abrams, their third partner and lead attorney with the firm, only took high profile cases. Picking up the file, she said, "You and I both know Roman is very select with the cases this firm takes on. Who the hell is this guy, Cris?"

Looking directly into Sophia's beautiful face, Cris let out a loud sigh. He secretly loved this woman and had from the moment he met her. However, she didn't reciprocate the feelings. He hated that Sophia was being pulled into the middle of this, but he was stuck dealing with another big case. Plus, if he was being honest, Louie was the best prosecuting attorney on the planet. Cris saw the suspicion lighting her violet eyes and knew she was not going to like his answer. "His name is Aleksandr," Hallsey said as he watched her voluptuous body tense. "Aleksandr Volkov."

Across town, Nikolai Volkov bent over the pool table in the luxurious game room as he shot the ball, missing the corner pocket. Standing up to look at his older brother, he said, "What the hell are we going to do, Zan? I don't understand how this could be happening!"

Downing his glass of whiskey, Aleksandr walked to the table to take his shot. He couldn't believe he was being accused of murdering Viktor. After reluctantly leaving the loveliest creature he had ever seen at Andrei's establishment, he had made his way back to his suite at the Ritz Carlton. However, he had been intercepted by NYC police in the lobby and had been taken downtown to the station. They had immediately informed him that Viktor was dead and he was the prime suspect. Not only was he the prime suspect, but they had found the proposed murder weapon in his suite, along with other clues pointing to him as the killer. Due to Aleksandr's notorious reputation and diplomatic ties, the police had treated him with kid gloves and had recommended he contact his attorney. The blond billionaire had not called his best friend and attorney, Artem Smirnov, because the man had shown up with his brother Nikolai and a whole team of security. Unfortunately, the international media had already caught wind of the fiasco, and Artem had recommended he dodge them by staying in his suite, at least until they had time to think.

Pulling back his stick, the grey-eyed billionaire let out a sigh as he shot two balls into a side pocket. He could not believe Viktor had been murdered. Viktor had taken in Aleksandr and his brother after his own father and mother had died. The older Russian man had been his father's lifelong best friend and had been forced to hide the siblings underground at one point because the bratva leader who had killed their father, wanted the entire Volkov family dead and rotting in the ground. Viktor had enacted vengeance against his father's killer and had instantly made Aleksandr the new leader of the Volkov family. He was now thirty-eight and one of the most powerful men in the world. In that time, Aleksandr and his brother had cleaned up a large portion of the mafia underworld and had made their business an international corporation.

Hitting another ball into a corner pocket, Aleksandr stood up and ran an agitated hand through his dirty-blond hair. "Someone is trying to fuck with me, Nikolai, and I don't like it. This little stunt simply confirms my suspicions. How else would you explain the bloody weapon in my room or the fact that they knew I was meeting with Viktor? If I were a betting man, I would put my money on Morrison."

"That asshole is a coward, Zan, who should have died a long time ago. He beats his wife and lives behind her name. You really think Paul has the balls to be behind this mess?" Nikolai asked, sitting on the edge of the pool table. How dare someone attempt to hurt his brother! His brother might be one deadly bastard, but he was also a compassionate, loving, and generous man.

"Yes, I do. We just need to see where he was when all of this went down," Aleksandr calmly replied as he sunk the last ball into the hole. When his eyes met Nikolai's, however, they were dark with emotion. "As for the time being, my dear brother, you will be tucked away safely in Moscow. I want you flying back there tonight."

"Bullshit!" Nikolai shouted as his own darkened grey eyes narrowed. "I don't need a damn babysitter, Zan, and I certainly don't need to be hidden away at home. I think I can take care of myself. You've taught me how to use a gun, remember? I've saved your lousy ass more than once."

Aleksandr chuckled loudly at Nikolai's remark as he walked over to where his brother sat on the pool table. Nikolai had the Volkov grey eyes, but his hair was coal black, and he was clean shaven. Physically, the younger man was a couple inches smaller in stature, at six-foot-four, and had a leaner, although muscular build. He was extremely handsome, though, and Nikolai was forever the quintessential ladies' man. Women flocked to his brother who was softer, kinder, and much funnier than Aleksandr. The older sibling had personally gone to great lengths to protect Nikolai from ending up like him. So far, he had been able to do just that.

Gripping the back of Nikolai's head affectionately, Aleksandr found his brother's annoyed face. "Look, just humor me, okay? I know you can take care of yourself, but I would never forgive myself if something happened to you."

The younger man rolled his eyes at her brother's tone. Although he had a soft smile on his face, Aleksandr was deadly serious. Nikolai loved his brother, but sometimes he could be too overbearing and protective. "So, I leave for home tonight?"

"Yes," Aleksandr replied, pleased with Nikolai's consensus to his demands. Taking a seat beside his brother on the pool table, Aleksandr said, "As soon as you land, I need you to check on Viktor's wife. Our men are guarding her every move as we speak. I have no doubts that whoever killed Viktor will try to kill her too."

"I can't believe Viktor is dead, Zan," Nikolai said, a deep sadness creeping into his grey eyes as he looked at his brother. "He didn't deserve to die like that. Poor Anya. Have you spoken with her? I can't even imagine how she is feeling right now."

"She was inconsolable when I spoke to her yesterday," Aleksandr replied, stretching out his legs as he rubbed his neatly trimmed beard. It had almost broken him to hear Viktor's wife sobbing over the loss of her husband and daughter. "Today, was not much better."

Nikolai could not imagine losing a loved one, especially his older brother. The thought of losing Aleksandr had an intense ache forming in the center of his chest. "Zan," the ebony-haired man began quietly. "Are you worried about being accused of murder? I mean, what if we can't get you out of this mess? This attack seems personal and well thought out. If something happened to you—"

"Niki, I need you to look at me," Aleksandr replied, reaching out to grip the back of his brother's neck lovingly. "I'm not worried about being accused of this crime, and neither should you be. I didn't kill Viktor, and everyone in the underworld knows it. I just need to find the fucker who did. You trust me, don't you?"

---

Aleksandr squeezed Nikolai's neck as he watched his brother's eyes moisten. He rubbed the nape as he comforted Nikolai, to reassure him that everything was going to be all right. Truth be told, he really wasn't concerned about being framed for Viktor's murder. Not only had he not killed Viktor, but Aleksandr owned too many individuals in high places who would ensure he would never be convicted of a parking ticket, let alone murder. The sadness weighing on his soul tonight was for Viktor's wife and daughter. If he was in danger, so were they. Aleksandr would die before he let anyone hurt them or endanger the empire he had built. He hated moments like this because he felt alone and vulnerable.

"You know I do, Zan," Nikolai replied sincerely. "But I also know that you tend to carry the weight of the world on your shoulders, big brother. You don't always have to do that. You can stumble. I'll catch you."

Nikolai's words had a small smile touching Aleksandr's mouth. When his parents had died, it had been his job to step in and be a father of sorts to his younger brother. Nikolai, who was now thirty, always had a smile on his handsome face and was Aleksandr's most trusted confidant. He always put the family first but was a ruthless shark when it came to business and making money. Aleksandr couldn't be prouder of his younger brother, and the two siblings were as thick as thieves.

Touched by Nikolai's words, Aleksandr pulled him in for a loving embrace. Releasing the younger man, he smiled and winked. "I'll keep that in mind. Now, if you're done nursing me from your tit, Mama, I would like to see what information you found out about the prosecutor in my case."

Flipping off his brother, Nikolai said, "Apparently, this lawyer is one of the best in the world. Hasn't lost a case, from what I understand, a real ruthless jerk."

"So, I've heard. What's his name?"

"Louie Rousseau." Nikolai grinned, shaking his head at Aleksandr's blasé attitude. "Shouldn't you know the name of the attorney who wants to lock you up and throw away the key?"

"Louie," Aleksandr scoffed in disgust as he rolled his grey eyes. "Sounds like a fucking used car salesman. Like I said, dear brother, meeting with the attorney at the deposition in a couple days is nearly a formality. I've got everything under control. See what else you can find on this prick and see what price it will take to pay him off. Now, if you will excuse me, I have another meeting that I must attend, and you have a plane to catch."

"A meeting, huh?" Nikolai asked, knowing full well what his brother was implying. "And what is her name? Did you meet her last night at Nona?"

Thinking about the remarkable, beautiful redhead from the night before, had a sensual smile tugging the corners of Aleksandr's mouth. "Da, I did. Her sub name is El, and just so you know, I'm bringing her back to Russia with me, but she will not be yours for the taking, brother. This woman will belong solely to me."

"What?" Nikolai said in mock horror, but he was intrigued at the serious look on his brother's bearded face. "You always share your women with me, Zan. You know I was just at Andrei's a few days ago. How do you know I didn't already sleep with her?"

"Because if you had seen this woman, little brother, you would not have let her go," Aleksandr said, raising his eyebrows up and down comically at Nikolai.

"Damn, Zan! Now, I am curious! I at least get to look, right? Shouldn't you at least know the woman's real name before you move her into your home?"

Aleksandr flipped his brother off as the younger man laughed out loud before he exited the room. The blond billionaire hated that he did not know El's real name, but things had not gone as planned last night. Aleksandr had talked with Andrei briefly this morning, to find out further personal information about the woman, but his friend had been unable to find anything else on her. All he knew was that El had better be at the club tonight. Even with all the drama happening in his life today, Aleksandr had been unable to shake her from his thoughts. To make matters worse, he could still smell her on his skin and taste her sweet, intoxicating scent on his tongue. Tonight, he planned on losing himself inside the violet-eyed vixen. Tomorrow, he would focus on the Viktor situation.

# Chapter 4

S ophia sat at the huge mahogany desk in her upscale New York office, as she meticulously reviewed the large stack of files laid out before her. Feeling overwhelmed and a headache coming on, she let out a soft sigh and stretched her slender neck from side to side. Sliding off her black glasses, Sophia pinched the bridge of her nose and closed her eyes a moment. This Volkov case was already becoming a huge pain in her ass, and she hadn't even met with the deposition team yet. There was little to no personal information on the Russian businessman, and what she had found left her with a bad taste in her mouth. Aleksandr Volkov was a criminal, plain and simple, who pretended to be a diplomat and legit business owner. She had never lost a case and had sent the most despicable of men to prison, but this guy took things to a whole other level. Why had her colleagues suggested she handle this case? It was looking to Sophia like the case against Aleksandr was pretty cut and dried, and she would love to send the man who murdered Viktor Sergei away.

"Louie, sorry to bother you again, but I got the file you

wanted earlier," the young, blonde secretary said, interrupting Sophia's thoughts as she entered the room. "Don't take offense, but you look tired. Are you sure I can't get you anything?"

Sophia let out a loud sigh as she stood up to stretch out her slender frame. Truth be told, she had been unable to sleep since meeting the Russian Dom. When she wasn't focused on the high-profile murder case, her thoughts were on him. When Sophia was in bed, she spent time masturbating instead of sleeping. Looking at the secretary, she asked, "Actually, can you get me a couple of Tylenol, Corinne? I've got a horrible headache brewing." When she took the small glass of water and pills from her secretary a few minutes later, she queried, "Still no call from Volkov's attorney? That asshole was supposed to call me this morning, but I haven't heard from him. That sense of entitlement is exactly why I hate dealing with the uber rich sometimes."

"Still no calls, babe." Corinne chuckled as she took the glass from Sophia and walked over to place it back on the drink cart. When she came back, she asked in concern, "Are you sure you want to be referring to Volkov's attorney as an asshole? From what I've heard on the telly, he and those associated with him are not the kind of men you want to be calling names."

"Men like Volkov don't scare me. Given his current position, I can call him whatever I please. After all, I plan on sending his ass to prison for life, or better yet, to the electric chair," Sophia scoffed, rolling her soft violet eyes.

"Mmm, but what an ass to send away!" the young secretary replied seductively as she licked her lips, imagining the man in question. When Sophia looked at Corinne in disbelief, she said, "Come on, Louie! Surely, you've seen a picture of Aleksandr Volkov. The man is sinfully delicious and completely unattached. I would run my tongue all over that body if he asked me to. Who knows? Maybe the two of you could work out a deal if money somehow becomes an issue. He's hot; you're hot. I say fuck the shit out him and call it a day!"

"You are such a slut, Corinne!" Sophia exclaimed laughingly. "Look, I've seen pictures of Mr. Volkov and I'm not that impressed. He's attractive, I will give you that, but I'm not into black-haired men. The guy is a little too metro for me. I like them a little on the scruffy side and bigger. Our relationship will be strictly professional, I can assure you."

"Not impressed?" Corinne shrieked in mock outrage. "I'm not sure what pictures you are looking at, but we clearly are not talking about the same man. The Aleksandr I've seen is blond, big, and positively gorgeous! No wonder you're single, Louie. You have zero taste when it comes to men."

Sophia responded to the secretary's comment by flipping her off. Before the red-haired attorney said another word, she glanced at the clock on the wall and shouted, "Oh shit! It's almost two, and I meet with Volkov and his attorney in about an hour. Would you call and let them know I'm on my way and that I might be a little late? I'll give Roman a call in the car." She then stood up and threw the laptop and files in her briefcase and quickly headed out the door.

Almost an hour later, across town in the district courthouse, Aleksandr sat in a conference room with his attorney Artem and a handful of other men. He was pissed and ready to walk the fuck out the door. The prosecuting attorney was late, and he absolutely hated incompetence. How dare that bastard Louie leave him waiting! Didn't he realize it wasn't wise to upset a man who was already in a dark, foul mood? Since being stood up by El the other night, Aleksandr was ready to kill someone, and he didn't really care who it was. Looking at Roman Abrams, who sat directly across from him, he barked loudly, "I'm giving your guy two more minutes to arrive. If he doesn't show, then I'm leaving. I don't have time for this shit!"

Before Roman could respond to Aleksandr, the door swung open and in walked Sophia. Putting her briefcase on the table and turning off her phone, she herself was angry and extremely irritated. Damn traffic! Not only was traffic horrible, but Sophia had gotten a speeding ticket. Without glancing up, she pulled out her files and quickly said, "Gentlemen, I am so sorry I'm late. I can assure everyone that being late is not a typical behavior for me. Let's get down to business, shall we? I've wasted enough of your time."

---

When Sophia's remarks were met with silence, she looked up and lost her breath immediately. Her violet eyes focused on the strikingly handsome man in an expensive, dark gray suit as she froze. What in the hell was the dominant from Nona doing sitting across from her? He was staring at her with the same surprised look. Feeling her nipples harden in arousal, Sophia watched a smile cross his gorgeous face as he leaned his massive, muscular body back casually against the chair and crossed his arms over his broad chest. Her pussy walls began to pulse as eyes that almost appeared silver scanned every inch of her body and a sensual smile touched his full, pink lips. The man who had been plaguing her dreams was now sitting in front of her and even more delicious than she remembered. Sophia wanted to undress Aleksandr and run her hands along the well-defined abdomen and thighs that she knew lay beneath the expensive, Armani linen.

Seeing the color drain from Sophia's face, Roman stood up and asked in her ear, "You okay, Lou? Is something wrong?"

"Y-yeah… I'm sorry," Sophia stammered suddenly as she blinked, breaking eye contact with Aleksandr. The picture of the Volkov man in her file had clearly been wrong. She could not believe Aleksandr Volkov was the same Alek she had been intimate with at Nona. What the hell was she going to do? She needed time to think! "Look, I'm sorry to keep you guys waiting, but I need a moment. Excuse me."

---

Aleksandr watched a very flustered and almost panicked El walk out of the room and slam the door behind herself. He fought the urge to jump up out of his chair and follow her. The Russian was torn between wanting to swoop her up in his arms and beating her ass for disobeying him the other night by not showing up. Not only had he destroyed Andrei's private room at the club, but he had his men scour the city looking for her. Unfortunately, his men had found nothing, but then he hadn't had much to go on. Yet here she was, in the flesh, the prosecuting attorney in his case. Fate really had a fucked-up sense of humor sometimes.

Sensing his friend's inner turmoil and feeling the intensity of emotions rolling off him in waves, Artem leaned over to whisper in Russian, "Everything all right, Zan? Do you know her?"

"That's the beautiful submissive I had the pleasure of tasting the other night," Aleksandr replied in his native tongue. "I have been searching the whole damn city for her little ass, and here she walks in, ready to throw the book at me."

"The case is over then," Artem said, a smile lighting his handsome face. "She's your alibi. If you were fucking her, then you couldn't have been killing Viktor. I say in light of this new information, we recuse the case and head back to Moscow."

"In time, Artem, in time," Aleksandr said, rubbing his bearded chin in thought. "I want to see what she does first."

"Zan, as not only your friend, but as your attorney, I would have to advise against that. I don't think that's a good idea."

"Since when have I cared what you thought?" The blond billionaire chuckled, looking affectionately at Artem. When the attorney shot him a 'go to hell' look, Aleksandr said in a serious tone, "Look, I know you care about me, all right. Let's just play this out. I want to see how my little pigeon handles herself under pressure."

"Fine, but if she has some sort of personal vendetta against you, then I'm calling it."

"Of course," Aleksandr replied calmly seconds before Sophia walked back into the room. He stifled a grin when she intentionally avoided his gaze and began fooling with her laptop. To gain her attention, Aleksandr slammed his fist down on the table. When her eyes met his, he asked in a deep, raspy voice, "Who the hell are you, sweetheart? We have been waiting patiently for a man by the name of Louie Rousseau, and I don't believe you're him. Are you his secretary?"

Aleksandr hungrily licked his lips as his eyes scanned the body of the stunning goddess standing across the table. He loved the range of emotions he saw sweeping across her lovely, radiant face. He had traveled the world and slept with hundreds of women, but he could not get over how ravishing the deep, magenta-red haired woman was. The billionaire felt his dick stir to life in his pants as his eyes made their way up toned, shapely calves to wide, thick hips, then up farther, to her porcelain face. He stifled a moan at the way the white, button up linen top hugged her breasts and the mid-thigh, black skirt that hugged her perfect heart-shaped ass. The woman was built like an hourglass, but as beautiful as her body was, it didn't compare to her exquisite looks. Aleksandr felt drawn to this woman and found himself leaning toward her across the table as he anticipated her response. He really was curious as to how she would proceed with this case, especially since the two had been intimate.

"I can assure you, Mr. Volkov, that I am Louie Rousseau," Sophia said, watching the man's eyes scan her body like a lion intently watching its prey. Her heart skipped a beat as his masculine, clean scent washed over her.

"Bullshit!" Aleksandr scoffed, as her eyes narrowed. He loved the way she lifted her head defiantly and met his gaze head on. "What's your real name, sweetheart? There is no way your name is Louie!"

———

Sophia felt an electric shock run down her spine as he leaned even closer toward her, across the table. She knew he was playing with her, and she didn't like it. Sophia had decided in the hallway that she would play along with the case until she figured out how to tell Roman about her indiscretion. The violet-eyed beauty wanted nothing more than to run her hands up Alek's big, muscular body and smash her lips to his, but she knew sleeping with him was a conflict of interest. Her whole career potentially hung in the balance by one night of debauchery on her part, and Sophia wasn't about to lose her livelihood to a Russian thug.

Shaking her head, the alabaster-skinned woman straightened her back indignantly, took a deep breath, and looked directly into the billionaire's eyes. "If you must know, Mr. Volkov, my full name is Sophia Elouise Rousseau. Not that it's any of your business, but Louie is a nickname that I was given in law school by one of my professors. I can assure you that I am a woman and very capable of handling this case."

A vein pulsed in Aleksandr's thick, corded neck at Sophia's dismissive tone as she demurely took a seat in her chair and began typing on her laptop. There was no way in hell he was going to let a woman dismiss him like that. Who did this woman think she was? Aleksandr may be sexually attracted to her, but he would be damned if he let her talk to him like that. Reaching across the table, he closed the laptop Sophia was typing on. His grey eyes darkened into slits as he growled, "Is that so? I suggest if you want to keep your job that I'm sure you fucked a man to get, then you apologize to me."

Sophia gasped loudly in disbelief as she stared incredulously at Aleksandr. She was torn between anger, shock, and lust as she swallowed the lump in her throat and licked her lips. As Aleksandr's gaze dropped from her eyes to her mouth, she felt her clit begin to pulse with need as wetness seeped onto her underwear. Shaking herself mentally, Sophia inwardly chastised herself for her behavior. Aleksandr Volkov may be used to making women bow at his feet, but she wasn't the ordinary, everyday female. Sophia let no man control her, and Aleksandr certainly wouldn't be the first.

Clearing her throat and crossing her legs demurely, Sophia looked directly into the billionaire's eyes. However, before she could tell Aleksandr where he could get off, she heard Roman say loudly, "Mr. Volkov, let me be the first to apologize for Ms. Rousseau's behavior. Clearly, she is not feeling like herself today, and this was the first time she has ever been late to a deposition. I should have clarified that Louie, or Sophia, is a woman, but I assumed her gender would not be an issue. However, if you and your attorney Artem feel that a different prosecutor is needed, then we will reschedule this deposition and I will assign another associate to the case. What would you like to do?"

Aleksandr did not respond as he sat and watched the redhead. He loved the defiant gleam in her eyes as she stared at him angrily. The only thing he could do right now was fight the urge to drag the tempting woman across the table and fuck the hell out of her! He had nearly come unglued when she licked her lips and began nibbling on them. Never in his life, had he lost control with a woman, yet here he was, acting like a raving lunatic! Without sparing a glance at Roman, he said in a deep, masculine voice void of emotion, "Ms. Rousseau can stay if she can maintain her attitude and composure. I would like to hear an apology from her lips, though, before we get started; enough time has been wasted."

Sophia would rather take a beating than say 'I'm sorry' to Aleksandr Volkov! The man was pompous, arrogant, maddening, and simply put... an asshole! Closing her eyes a moment to gain her composure and control her emotions, Sophia took a deep breath. When she opened them, she looked directly at Aleksandr and said through clenched teeth, "I'm sorry, Mr. Volkov. Now can we please get down to business?"

Aleksandr leaned back casually in his chair as a pleased, smug smile lit his gorgeous, bearded face. "Thank you, Ms. Rousseau." He grinned, his voice deeply masculine and sensual. "I'm glad to see that you can be... submissive."

"I can assure you Ms. Rousseau will be professional," Roman interjected quickly before looking directly at the stenographer. "Felix, let's begin."

Artem leaned over to whisper in Aleksandr's ear, "Maybe we should request another prosecuting attorney, Zan. I just received a text that Sophia's firm has represented Viktor's daughter in the past. That, coupled with your interlude the other night, would clearly get her dismissed on the grounds of prejudice."

"No," Aleksandr replied coolly, licking his lips as he hungrily and openly stared at Sophia. "I want her to stay."

"Alek, as your best friend, I think it would be a good idea—"

"Start the questions," Aleksandr said loudly, looking at Roman a moment, cutting off Artem's words.

Sophia began the deposition by asking him basic demographic information. As Roman took over and moved into questions about the actual case, she was unnerved at the way Aleksandr's eyes roamed over her body. He also appeared at times, to be studying her face intently. Taking a deep breath, she pulled her violet eyes from his and went back to taking notes on her legal pad.

Aleksandr answered Roman's mundane questions with little thought. The only thing racing through his mind was the incredible beauty sitting across from him. Sophia Rousseau had to be the loveliest woman alive. Aleksandr could tell the intensity of his gaze was unsettling her and that kept the sensual smile on his face. Sophia's skin was flawless, and her neck was long and slender. Peeking out of the white top she wore, was the valley of her breasts when the woman shifted a certain way. Aleksandr remembered what those perfect breasts looked like naked and he wanted to run his tongue along that valley before burying his bearded face between them. *Fuck, get it together, man,* he thought to himself. *This is the woman who defied you the other night and may want you rotting in a prison.*

"Mr. Volkov, we are going to move into the night Mr. Sergei was murdered," Roman said as he looked at Sophia. "Louie, if you please."

"Mr. Volkov, is it true that Mr. Sergei asked you to meet him the evening he was murdered?" Sophia asked, leaning back in her chair and crossing her legs.

"Yes, Viktor asked me to meet him for dinner," Aleksandr said, leaning back in his own chair.

"What exactly did the two of you talk about?"

"We engaged in small talk before Viktor discussed me taking over leadership of his business."

"Did the conversation become heated at some point?"

"Yes," the wealthy blond man countered simply, before Artem leaned over to whisper something in his ear.

"Is it true that you cursed at Mr. Sergei and threw a table and chair as he left the restaurant? This doesn't sound like the actions of a man just asked to take over a multi-million-dollar business, Mr. Volkov."

"It is if that man doesn't want it," Aleksandr replied as he saw a moment of surprise flash in the depths of Sophia's eyes. She clearly had not been expecting that. "I also won't deny I raised my voice or lost my temper with Viktor, but he was anticipating that."

"Is the argument you had with Mr. Sergei the reason he left the restaurant? Eyewitnesses report that he looked frazzled and upset when he left. Would you agree with those details?"

"No, I wouldn't. Viktor left because he received word that his daughter Kira was in some sort of trouble. There also was no argument between the two of us. He wanted me to do something, and I refused," Aleksandr said, shrugging his wide shoulders.

Sophia hated to admit it, but there was something about Aleksandr's demeanor that told her he was telling the truth. "What was wrong with his daughter Kira?"

"He didn't say, and I didn't ask," Aleksandr responded, fingering his chin as Artem leaned over and whispered in his ear again. "The reason seems rather irrelevant, doesn't it?"

"No, actually," Sophia replied, her violet eyes narrowing with disgust, "since Kira was murdered alongside her father, I would say what was wrong with her was quite relevant. Let's talk about the details of their murders, shall we? I'm sure you are aware, Mr. Volkov, that they were stabbed to death. Deaths related to stabbing are typically very personal and an act of rage. The weapon found at the crime scene has your fingerprints on it. Why is that?"

"I don't know. Since I wasn't present at the scene, I would assume someone is trying to connect me to the crime," Aleksandr said very matter of factly.

"If you were not present at the scene of the crime, can you tell us where you were?"

"I was at a night club, eating the pussy of a very delicious submissive named El, if you must know." Aleksandr smiled, unbuttoning his designer suit jacket and relaxing back in his chair. He loved the glint of anger and panic he saw momentarily leap into Sophia's eyes. She was secretly praying he would not announce that she was the submissive. When the redhead looked at him pleadingly, Aleksandr asked, "Do you speak any other languages, Ms. Rousseau?"

Looking at Aleksandr with uncertainty in her eyes, Sophia replied, "Yes, but why does that matter?"

"Just curious. What other languages do you speak?"

With a loud sigh as she rolled her eyes, Sophia said, "French and Spanish."

"Are you married, Sophia?" Aleksandr asked in French, watching her intently.

"No, I'm not, Mr. Volkov," Sophia responded in the same language, totally taken off guard by his question. "How is that question even relevant to this case?"

*Damn, I want this woman,* Aleksandr thought to himself. He could tell how fiery and passionate Sophia was, by the way she looked at him and how quick her responses were. She also was pretending to be unaffected by him, but Aleksandr knew otherwise. He felt the sexual chemistry and electricity coming off the woman in waves. "Tell me, sweet one," Aleksandr continued in French. "Do I make you uncomfortable? I think I do."

"No, you actually disgust me," Sophia replied simply, averting her gaze slightly from him.

"I do believe that's the second lie I've heard escape those luscious lips. The first one was when you told me that you would meet me at Andrei's club two nights ago. Just so you know, there will be a punishment for lying."

"Punishment? Yeah, right," Sophia scoffed, averting his gaze but feeling the heat he was emitting across the table. "Look, I am not about to take time away from this deposition to discuss what happened between us at Andrei's club."

"Don't you dare dismiss me, pet!" Aleksandr said between clenched teeth heatedly as her eyes flew to his. "I know I didn't have time to set the ground rules with you the other night, but you will not be disrespectful to me. Do I make myself clear? I don't want to have to punish you here, but I will."

There was something in Aleksandr's body language and eyes that told Sophia he would not hesitate to punish her, would even enjoy it. Lowering her lavender eyes, she quickly offered, "I wasn't trying to be disrespectful to you, Mr. Volkov—"

"Alek… and look at me when you speak to me."

"Alek," Sophia corrected herself, her eyes once again meeting his. She hated the twinkle of pleasure she saw in their silver depths. "As I was saying, I am not trying to be rude to you, but now isn't the time to discuss our sexual involvement. I just want to finish this deposition, all right?"

"Sophia has to be the most tantalizing woman I've ever seen, Artem," Aleksandr said to his best friend in French but kept his eyes on her. "I can tell you, friend, she tastes as good as she looks, better, actually. I would give my right fucking arm to run my tongue between those gorgeous breasts at this very moment."

Sophia felt her pussy constrict and pulse as it flooded with her juices at Aleksandr's words. She could feel her chest swell with the knowledge that this gorgeous man still wanted her. Although Sophia wouldn't admit it, she wanted him too. She wanted to straddle Aleksandr's lap and ride him hard. She wanted his massive, tattooed hands all over her body, but this man was the enemy, and she was stuck between a rock and a hard place.

"Mr. Volkov, if you are going to continue to speak to Ms. Rousseau in another language, then I recommend we get an interpreter in here, so everyone is privy to the conversation," Roman interjected, seeing the blush creep across Sophia's face. He could tell whatever Aleksandr was saying was making his partner uncomfortable. Leaning over, he whispered to her, "I don't know what the hell is going on with you, Louie, but you had better get it together."

Aleksandr watched Roman whisper in Sophia's ear, and he didn't like the anger he saw light their purple depths. Clearly, Roman said something to piss her off. Switching to Russian, Aleksandr leaned over to Artem to say in a low voice, "Contact Ivan. I want him to do a background check on Ms. Rousseau. I want to know every bit of information that he can find on her."

"Zan, you shouldn't be playing around with this woman," Artem replied, rubbing his eyes as he shook his head. "I get that you're sexually attracted to her, but she is one of the country's top prosecuting attorneys. She clearly doesn't like you—"

"Oh, I beg to differ." Aleksandr smiled, ignoring Artem's warning. "Sophia wants me just as much as I want her. Plus, I can see in her eyes that she knows I'm innocent. She just doesn't know what to do with that information yet. I can help her figure it out."

"Oh my god, I didn't just hear you say that!" Artem exclaimed, running an agitated hand through his dark brown hair. Aleksandr was more like a brother to him than a friend and he loved the man dearly. However, once the billionaire had his mind set on something, there was no changing it, no matter how dangerous Artem thought it was.

At that moment, Sophia motioned for the stenographer to begin taking notes once again. Just as she did, she watched Aleksandr stand up and button his designer jacket. She demurely crossed her legs and asked, "Mr. Volkov, do you need a break? If so, we can pause the proceedings."

"No, I'm ending this deposition. I have another meeting that I must attend. We will just have to continue this another time," Aleksandr stated in a matter of fact tone again, as he rounded the table with Artem. "Roman, your people call mine." He then leaned down beside Sophia, rubbed his bearded chin against her cheek, and inhaled her perfume. Fuck. she smelled amazing! "We have found ourselves in a very strange predicament." Aleksandr began in French. "If you want to know the truth about what happened to Viktor. Meet me tonight, at eight o'clock sharp. I'll forward my address to your secretary. Don't disappoint me again, pet. You won't like the consequences. Your safe word was pigeon, right?" A smile touched Aleksandr's lips when Sophia gasped. Nuzzling his nose against her cheek, he then intentionally let his hand run up her thigh. He let out a deep, sensual chuckle when the breath caught in her throat once again and she released what sounded like a soft moan. Aleksandr then rose and left the room with Artem in tow.

Sophia let out a shaky breath when she heard the door close behind her. The large Russian man had felt so damn good pressed against her that she had momentarily forgotten she was in a room full of her peers. Looking up, Sophia was not surprised to see everyone watching her. She was, however, surprised to see the look of rage disfiguring Roman's face. "Roman, I'm so sorry. Look, there is something that I need—"

"I can't fucking believe you, Louie!" Roman shouted as everyone else quickly began to leave the room. "I don't know what in the hell is going on with you today, but it had better be the first and only time I see this kind of behavior. You might have just cost us the case of a lifetime! Now get the hell out of here and go home! Get some sleep or something, and take tomorrow off!"

Tears sprang to Sophia's eyes as she said forcefully, "Roman, if you would just let me explain—"

"You can explain later. Right now, I'm too pissed at you to even listen. Now go home!"

Sophia inhaled deeply and threw her files and laptop in her bag. She blinked back tears and willed them to stop as she packed her things and headed toward the door. Her career as a lawyer was over, and she knew it. Maybe taking the rest of the day off would give her some time to come up with a plan on how to handle things. Grabbing her briefcase, Sophia said nothing further as she left the room and her future as an attorney.

## Chapter 5

The violet-eyed woman downed her glass of wine as she sat on the balcony of her expensive, downtown apartment. Pouring herself another one, she kicked back and gazed up at the blackened, starless sky. In the distance, she saw a flash of lightning and heard the loud clap of thunder and knew the thunderstorm was quickly approaching. Oh, how the weather mirrored her own life, she thought to herself as she took another drink of wine. What the hell was she going to do? Sophia had worked so hard for her career, and now thanks to one night of passion, it was over! Today, had been a complete, fucking disaster and Sophia really had no idea how she was going to get out of her current predicament. She knew Aleksandr had not personally killed Viktor Sergei because at the time of the alleged murder, he was with her. She still didn't know if Aleksandr had ordered the hit, but there was no way his prints could have been on the murder weapon at the scene. The only ethical thing for her to do was to tell Roman the truth, but in doing so, her career would be over. *So much for making partner at such an exclusive law firm,* Sophia thought to herself as she took another drink of wine. *Your life as you know it has ended, all thanks to Aleksandr Volkov.*

Feeling the first drops of rain hitting her skin, Sophia stood up with her glass of wine and quickly made her way into her apartment. Flopping down on the chaise lounge, she glanced at the clock on the wall—nine-thirty. She wondered what Aleksandr was doing at this very moment. Had he been upset when she hadn't shown up at his suite? *Of course not, you ninny,* she chided herself. *He probably has already filled his bed with someone else.* Sophia had considered going to his place and fucking the hell out of him, but then common sense had prevailed. The man was a dangerous thug with ties to the underworld, and although he may be disgustingly sexy, Aleksandr was not the type of guy she needed in her life right now. Yes, she could have the most amazing sex of her life, but that would only make matters worse in the long run. Sophia would already have a target on her back because of her brief association with Aleksandr, and she really didn't need the media attention that came along with that. For those reasons alone, Sophia had opted for staying home. Every fiber and nerve ending in her body had screamed otherwise, but she was going to listen to her head this time around.

Thinking of the deposition meeting today, had a mixture of dread and butterflies spreading across her petite frame. The butterflies she felt were all related to Aleksandr and his gorgeous body. Damn, if the man hadn't been over the top with his sexual prowess and energy. He had, again, made it clear how much he wanted her and what he wanted to do with her. As soon as Sophia had gotten home, she had masturbated and jumped into a cold shower. Even after the shower, she could still feel and smell Aleksandr on her skin. The man had looked positively scrumptious in his suit and she had wanted nothing more than to lie across the table that separated them and offer herself to him for the taking. The feeling of dread, however, was becoming more and more pronounced. Sophia had been unable to control her emotions or her tongue around Aleksandr and it didn't take a rocket scientist to figure out that something was going on between them. Roman had been furious with her and would fire her once he found out the truth. Good thing Sophia had money saved up, so she could move to another country. However, as high profile as this case was, she could kiss her career as a lawyer goodbye. Everyone would assume she was crooked and dirty, and worse than that, a whore. Plus, she had no doubt that her father and his legacy would be brought up. Why not add a little more fuel to the fire?

Sophia took another drink of wine when she felt the tears stinging the back of her eyes as she thought about her father. She had loved the man more than life itself and he had been good to her, but he was also an international criminal with a notorious reputation. Ethan Rousseau had not only been a drug lord, but a sort of murderer for hire. He had been wanted by the authorities in several countries, and his death had been celebrated by law officials and leaders of the underworld. Although many had hated her father, Sophia had loved him dearly. Yes, he had many faults and was not a good man in the eyes of the world, but as a father, he had been the greatest. He loved her unconditionally and taught her how to strive and survive. For a killer, Sophia's father had been so gentle and loving with her and her brother. Their childhood, although anything but normal, had been wonderful. When Ethan had been murdered, he had ensured that his children would never want for anything monetarily. She still had a large portion of the money her father had left her tucked away for a rainy day. Realistically, Sophia would never have to work again and would still live comfortably the rest of her life, but that simply wasn't her style. It was a big world and Sophia had no doubt she could start over again. She just didn't necessarily want to. Truth be told, Sophia had no real friends outside of work, so she really wouldn't be missed by many, if anyone.

Wiping the tears that dared to roll down her cheeks, Sophia knew there was only one way out of her situation. She would just have to tell the truth. There was no way in hell she was going to let an innocent man go to jail for something he didn't do. It appeared to her that Aleksandr was set up, and she had no idea why. She knew he was involved in the underbelly side of crime, but to what extent, she didn't know. Regardless of Aleksandr's criminal affiliations, she couldn't let him go to trial for the murder of Viktor Sergei. Plus, Aleksandr certainly didn't have the hands of a ruthless killer. Quite the opposite, really. Could a man who had brought her so much pleasure the other night be that bad? Shaking herself mentally, Sophia again chastised herself. *Aleksandr Volkov is the enemy! He is no more than a stranger off the street to you. You are only having these thoughts because he is the most gorgeous man on the planet. Get it together, Louie!*

Taking another drink of wine, Sophia was surprised to hear the ringing of the doorbell. *Must be the pizza I ordered,* she thought to herself as she made her way to the door. Opening it, Sophia froze in shock when she saw Aleksandr standing in her doorway dressed in a pair of jeans and a grey t-shirt, holding a bottle of expensive vodka. Her initial reaction was to slam the door on him, but the giant Russian anticipated her movements and wedged his body in the door so she couldn't close it. "Don't come in here, dammit! Go away!"

"We need to talk," Aleksandr said with a calm exterior and voice, but he was anything but on the inside. His dick hardened instantly as his eyes feasted on the pink, off the shoulder sweatshirt she wore and the skimpy, pink polka dot shorts. Her hair was pulled back in a loose ponytail and she wore red-rimmed glasses on her face. Fuck! Even casual, the woman was stunning! "Let me in, Sophia. I can help you if you let me in."

"Help me?" Sophia gasped, followed by a derisive laugh. "It's because of you that my career is over, Aleksandr! You can't help me. No one can."

Feeling a twinge of guilt at her words, Aleksandr softened his tone a bit as he said, "I didn't intentionally put you in this situation, sweetheart, but maybe together, we can figure a way out of it. Let me in, sweet one. I want to help."

With a loud sigh, Sophia loosened her grip on the door and allowed Aleksandr to walk into her apartment. As she walked toward the couch, she said over her shoulder, "You've got five minutes. Say your piece and get out."

Aleksandr watched Sophia walk over to table, where she picked up a glass of wine and downed it before she sat Indian style on the couch. His eyes scanned her apartment quickly, and he liked what he saw. By looking at her belongings, Sophia appreciated modern style and art the same as he did. He also liked the soft, feminine touches he found littering the large space. No one could mistake the fact that a woman lived here. His eyes then drifted back to the woman in question. Damn, her body was amazing, and her face was flawless without makeup. He had every intention of taking her to his bed tonight, but first, they needed to talk. Aleksandr just hoped his hormones could hold out long enough for the latter.

Sophia felt a blush cross her chest, neck, and face as Aleksandr studied her body. She watched him adjust the semi-soft erection in his jeans before he started to sit his massive frame into the small, stylish chair. When she felt her vaginal walls contract with need, she blurted out, "No need to get comfortable. You're not going to be staying that long."

Aleksandr simply smiled at her as he sat down anyway and leaned toward her, putting his elbows on his thighs. He then placed the bottle of vodka on the table sitting between them as he said, "Why don't you get us a couple glasses? I think both of us could use a drink."

Needing a drink herself, Sophia made her way to the kitchen and came back with two small glasses. "One drink, then we're done."

Pouring the clear, expensive liquid, Aleksandr asked, "Were you expecting company tonight? By the way you answered the door, I take it I was not the person you had anticipated."

"No, I ordered a pizza and thought you might be the delivery guy. What the hell are you doing here anyway?" Sophia asked abruptly, taking the glass of vodka from him. After watching him take a drink of the liquid, she also took a sip. She gasped and coughed as the vodka burned her throat. Gaining her composure as he chuckled, she said. "Look, there is no reason for you to be here, Alek. I know you didn't kill Viktor because you were with me at Nona's. I'm not sure if you ordered the hit or not, but I do know there is no way your prints could be on the weapon at the time of murder. I'm going to tell Roman that we were together. I just want to figure out the best way to break it to him."

"You belong to Roman?" Aleksandr questioned heatedly, slamming his glass down on the table. "Is he your dominant?"

"Hell no!" Sophia yelled before a slight smile touched her full lips. "Roman is my partner in the firm. There is no way in hell I would sleep with him. I actually find the thought of that amusing and... gross. I mean, he is an attractive, older man but... eww!" When the tension and intensity suddenly left Aleksandr's body at her response, she asked, "Answer me this, Volkov. I know you didn't kill Viktor and his daughter with your own hands, but did you order the hit? By the way, this conversation is strictly between the two of us."

"No, I didn't, but I'm sure I know who did," Aleksandr answered honestly, his eyes locked with hers. "Viktor was like a father to me. My parents were murdered when I was younger, and he raised us like his own."

"Us?"

"My brother Nikolai and me. As I told you in the deposition, he wanted me to take over his business and I declined. Not to brag, pet, but I'm already worth a few billion. I don't need his money or the hassle of dealing with his shit. However, I am left to clean up the mess whether I like it or not."

"Wait. Why would you have to clean up after Viktor if you don't plan on taking over his business?"

"Because Viktor had already set things into motion. Plus, like I said, he is like a father to me, and I won't see his bratva fall into the hands of the person who slaughtered him."

"Who killed Viktor?"

"Paul Morrison, his son-in-law," Aleksandr replied between clenched teeth as he poured both of them another drink. He loved the way Sophia crinkled her nose when she was deep in thought. This woman wasn't only beautiful, but she was highly intelligent. He had received a file on her from Ivan and had been more than impressed with her history. He also had been a little surprised to see that her father had been an elite member of the notorious European under-world. No wonder Sophia was spirited and had control issues. She had grown up predominantly with only herself to depend on. That bit of knowledge made him even more attracted to her.

"Paul Morrison?" Sophia asked, thinking of where she had heard that name before. "Why is that name familiar, and why do you think he is the one who murdered Viktor?"

"Paul owned several companies here in America that became embroiled in a big money laundering scandal involving politicians. To keep him quiet and their reputations intact, they sent him to Europe. That is where he met and married Viktor's daughter, Kira. He has spent the last several years attempting to destroy what his father-in-law built."

Sophia remembered that scandal all too well, and their law firm had represented a handful of those men. They had taken innocent people for billions of dollars in retirement funds. Taking another sip of her vodka, she asked, "So I'm assuming Viktor hated Paul and had no intention of leaving his business to him. Why would he kill his wife, though, and why does he hate you so much?"

"In Russia, I am leader of the largest bratva and own several Fortune 500 companies. My brother and I are also the only thing standing between Paul running the underworld," Aleksandr replied coolly, loving the way she was processing the information given to her. He could tell that her body language toward him had changed and was more relaxed. "As for Kira, Paul never loved her. Since before their wedding, he has cheated on her and physically abused her. Not even sure why she married the bastard, but she did. Viktor was dying of cancer, and Kira was pregnant with his grandchild, although Viktor didn't know this. Viktor's hatred of Paul was common knowledge and Kira's baby would have gotten everything. She was actually going to tell Viktor about the pregnancy the night they both were killed."

"You think Paul killed his unborn child?" Sophia asked in surprise, pure disgust evident on her face. "What kind of monster would kill his own child? Why would he do that?"

"You have to understand the philosophy of a bratva, pet," Aleksandr replied, disgusted as well by Paul's actions, but wanting her to understand. "Family is everything. Paul is only related by marriage. Viktor would have ensured that Paul had access to none of the child's money. He only had access to Viktor's because of Kira."

"But you weren't Viktor's biological family, so why would he leave everything to you?"

"I'm like family. Bratva leaders can change their philosophy if they want." Aleksandr smiled, taking another drink of his vodka. "My father was Viktor's best friend. They were like brothers. Viktor ensured we kept access to what was rightfully ours."

"Okay, I see where you're going. Paul kills Viktor and Kira and pins it on you. With you in prison, that would only leave Nikolai to take care of. I'm assuming he probably had a plan for him as well."

"He did, but I have already personally taken care of that," Aleksandr said, not adding that in the past two days, he had ordered the killing of ten men associated with the plot to kill Nikolai. No one fucked with those he loved and lived to tell it. "It's because of you, Sophia, that I can definitely prove my innocence. I couldn't be killing someone if I was spending my free time inside you. You are my out, sweet one, and I want to return the favor and see to it that you come out of this unscathed as well."

"Yeah, well, my career as a lawyer is over. There is nothing that you can do to help me. I appreciate you wanting to, but you don't need to. I got myself into this mess, and I'll get myself out. I'm not a damn charity case," Sophia replied, downing the last of the vodka. She then stood up and abruptly said, "Look, I've got some work to do so I'm going to ask you to leave. You can show yourself out."

Aleksandr growled in annoyance when Sophia dismissed him once again. Shooting to his booted feet, the giant Russian stalked toward her. When he reached her, Aleksandr gripped her bare shoulder before he roughly turned her around. He then shoved her back against a wall and wrapped her legs around his muscular waist. "I've already told you not to dismiss me, pet, but you continue to defy me. You need to be taught a lesson, so you never disobey me again."

Sophia pushed against Aleksandr's chest and struggled in

his arms as she yelled, "Let go of me, dammit! Put me down!" However, before she could say another word, she was tossed over Aleksandr's shoulder as he walked to the couch. When he sat down on the couch, he threw her face down over his lap. "What the hell are you doing? Help!" Sophia then cried out as he pulled down her pants and his large, scarred hand connected hard with her bottom.

Aleksandr's cock slammed against the zipper of his jeans when he delivered the first blow. He felt her stiffen and grow eerily quiet when he hit her bare ass a second time. Aleksandr knew Sophia was angry at him, so he decided to change his tactic somewhat. He then began to massage the cheek he had just spanked before he leaned over to place a kiss there. Alek immediately felt Sophia's body relax and heard a soft moan escape her lips. His slender, scarred fingers then slid in between her vaginal lips and began to tweak and gently tug on her clitoris. As one hand manipulated and rubbed the hooded clit, his other hand came down again on her naked bottom. This time, Aleksandr chuckled when she bucked her hips and her pussy flooded with wetness.

"Did you like that, pet?" Aleksandr asked near her ear before placing soft kisses on her exposed shoulder. Trailing the kisses up her neck, he said softly, "You aren't supposed to like your punishment."

"Why are you punishing me?" Sophia asked in a whisper soft moan just as two of Aleksandr's fingers began sliding in and out of her core. She had never been spanked in her life and didn't think she would ever be a fan, but this man did it with such finesse and pleasure that every nerve ending of her body felt electrified. When his hand came down hard again on her bottom, she felt the clear, sticky fluid running down her inner thighs.

"You're being punished because I don't like lies and I don't like being dismissed. You have done both," Aleksandr replied as his hand came down on her bottom again. "Convince me that you will never do either again, and the punishment will stop."

"Convince you?" Sophia asked in confusion, Aleksandr's actions making it difficult for her to think. She gasped in delighted rapture when he added a third finger to the ones gliding in and out of her tight pussy canal as his hand came down again. She could feel her vaginal walls constricting as the pending orgasm grew in her core. Did she even want the punishment to stop?

"Yes, convince me. Say I will never dismiss you or lie to you again, Sir." Aleksandr smiled smugly. He knew she was on the verge of an orgasm, but there was no way in hell he was going to let her come yet. It amazed him how quickly Sophia had gone from not liking the punishment to wanting more. Placing another kiss on the reddened, hot skin of her bottom, he then trailed his tongue along the crack of her wide, apple-shaped ass. Aleksandr leaned back down to whisper hungrily in her ear, "After I hear the words, I will pick up where we left off at Nona's."

Again, he struck Sophia's bottom. Clearly, Aleksandr was not going to stop until she did as he had commanded. She had no doubt that he wasn't going to let her have an orgasm, either, and her body desperately needed a release. The stinging pain from her bottom and the building pleasure between her legs had her quickly yelling, "I will never dismiss you or lie to you again, Sir." Then, just to make sure he knew she was telling him the truth, she added, "I promise."

Aleksandr then instantly flipped her over and cradled her in his big, muscular arms. He nuzzled her neck and placed kisses along the pulse there before he whispered, "That was good, pet. You sound convincing enough, but how do I know I can trust you?"

Sophia crawled off his lap and knelt between legs the size

of tree trunks. She then ran her hands under the t-shirt he wore before pulling it over his head. Her eyes widened in pleasure at the large muscles and darkly tanned skin that was ornately decorated in colorful tattoos and light blond hair. She ran her hands over the rippled muscles in his chest and stomach and kneaded the hard skin. Her mouth watered as her lavender eyes scanned every inch. Without thought, she said in awe, "You are so big and gorgeous. I can't wait to feel you inside me."

Aleksandr shifted uncomfortably in his seat as his cock throbbed even more painfully in his jeans. Damn, her eyes were eating him alive! Aleksandr had always known he was an attractive man, but he secretly thanked his maker that Sophia liked what she saw. He gave her a few more minutes to explore his upper body before he grabbed her hands and brought her face to his. "I'm glad you like my body, sweetness. I like yours as well. Would you like to taste it?"

"Yes, Sir," Sophia said breathlessly before Aleksandr tried to capture her lips with his in a passionate kiss. She jerked her head to the side before he could claim her mouth. "I said no kissing. It's too personal."

The growl came from deep in Aleksandr's throat as he knotted her silky, red hair in his fist and jerked her mouth to his. He felt her small hands pushing against his chest, but he didn't care as his tongue mated with hers. After a moment of fighting, Aleksandr felt Sophia begin to return the kiss before he felt her hands knot into his own dirty-blond hair. Breaking the kiss, he hissed, "You will not deny me any piece of your body. Your lips, just like your pussy, belong to me now. Do you understand?"

"Y-yes," Sophia stammered as she felt her shirt go up and over her head before his mouth captured hers again.

Aleksandr passionately kissed her a few more minutes, then his lips trailed across her jaw to her ear. He pulled the lobe with his teeth before he licked the sensitive spot behind it. There, he huskily whispered, "Suck my dick, pet. I want to feel your mouth on me."

Sophia's hands dropped to the button of his jeans as she placed butterfly kisses across his chest and stomach. Reaching into his pants, she pulled out his huge cock and began to slowly stroke it with both hands. She rubbed her thumb over the precum oozing from the head before she slipped it into her mouth to suck off. Pulling her finger out of her mouth, she hungrily licked her lips and leaned up to place a kiss on his mouth. "You taste like cinnamon and honey. So yummy."

Aleksandr smiled warmly at Sophia before he guided her head back to his cock. His head fell back on the couch cushion when her hot, moist mouth slowly engulfed the large tip. His hips instinctually rose each time her lips slid down the length a little farther, and her hands stroked the silky skin. Fuck, her mouth was amazing! Aleksandr loved the innocent way Sophia struggled to take more of his cock deeper into her mouth. He almost shot his load when her tongue found his balls and she sucked them into her mouth and stroked the wide length at the same time. Needing to be inside Sophia's tight, wet cunt, Aleksandr grabbed her under her arms and pulled her up, so she straddled his lap. Capturing her lips once again, he positioned her vaginal opening on the head of his dick.

"Wait! We can't!" Sophia urged breathlessly against his lips as her hands played with the blond hair at the nape of his neck. "We need a condom."

"No, we don't," Aleksandr replied just as urgently, his hands massaging her breasts. "I'll pull out before I come. I need to feel all of you, pet."

"But we—" Sophia replied before her words were cut off by Aleksandr's mouth again and him easing her down the mushroom-shaped tip of his cock. She moaned loudly and her head fell back in ecstasy, as his giant dick stretched her pussy wide and he continued to insert more of himself inside her dripping wet core. Her juices flooded her pussy and easily lubricated his wide length. "Gawd, you feel so good!" Sophia moaned when she was fully embedded on his cock.

Aleksandr fought the need to fuck Sophia fast and hard, as he allowed her small frame time to accept his size. She had the tightest, wettest pussy of any woman he had ever been with. Sophia's hot core hugged him like a snug glove, and he loved the way her vaginal walls softly contracted around him. His little pigeon felt wonderfully amazing and she was so responsive to his touch. Aleksandr knew he should be wearing a condom with her, but he wanted to feel all of her, every delicious inch. Kissing her lips again before his tongue mated with hers, Aleksandr gripped her bottom and eased her pussy up his cock before he slid her back down, increasing the pace.

Sophia's body was on overload as she rode Aleksandr. She felt her impending orgasm building deep within her core as she bounced up and down on his dick. Every inch of her skin was electrified as his hands and lips roamed her skin. She had only been with three or four men in the past, but none of them had prepared her for the sensations she felt with this one. Her vaginal walls were stretched wide, due to his massive girth, but not uncomfortably so. Each time he slid her down his cock, the tip of the head hit her G-spot. Every time she tried to catch a breath, Aleksandr's mouth captured hers in a fiery, explosive kiss.

"Does my sweet one need a release?" Aleksandr asked, gripping her breasts in his hands as he allowed her to take over the speed and pace of their lovemaking. He could tell by the expressions on her lovely face and the tightening of her vaginal muscles around his shaft that she was close to an orgasm. Sophia was breathtaking to watch as she edged closer and closer and took from him what she needed. "Tell me you need to climax."

"Please, Sir. I need to come." Sophia heard herself almost purr as she wrapped her arms around his thick neck and fully embedded his cock before grinding her hips against his. Feeling the pressure intensify, she yelled, "Oh shit!"

"Come, pet. I want to feel you come on my dick," Aleksandr said huskily. Then, as if on command, Sophia screamed, and he felt her pussy contracting hard and fast around his massive length. He gritted his teeth together in a mixture of pleasure and pain as the beautiful redhead got off and her whole body jerked and shook against him. He could feel his own orgasm building as her tight, wet pussy milked his cock. He felt her nails digging into his broad shoulders and a stream of blood trickling down his back. He loved the way her juices ran down his cock and pooled on the jeans he still wore. This woman was breathtaking to watch and Aleksandr had a feeling he could watch her every day for the rest of his life.

Sophia felt like her body was exploding into a million pieces as the orgasm coursed through her petite frame. She thought she was going to pass out momentarily, but Aleksandr's strength kept her from slipping away. She rode the crest and fall of each delightful wave until her turbulent emotions began to subside and her body began to find its way through the haze Aleksandr had created. Opening her lavender eyes, she looked at him and smiled sensually. "That was amazing. It's now your turn to come, Sir. May I suck you off?"

"Yes, but I want you to take as much of me into your mouth as you can. Drink every drop." Aleksandr returned her smile before he gripped the back of her neck and brought her in for a hard kiss. Breaking away, a shiver ran through him when she pulled herself off his cock. He relaxed on the couch and laid his arms across the back of it as Sophia positioned herself between his legs. Precum oozed from his erect dick as she slowly and methodically began stroking him with both of her small hands. His stomach muscles contracted, and he moaned when her tongue circled the head before she took him in her mouth. This time, Sophia fucked him with her mouth wildly, each time taking him deeper and deeper. When Aleksandr heard Sophia gag a little on his cock, he commanded, "Relax your throat muscles, sweetness."

Sophia did as she was told and relaxed her throat. She wasn't sure how she was fitting the girth of him in her mouth, but she was, and Aleksandr tasted so damn good. She could tell by the look of raw, unadulterated pleasure on his face and the way his hands were running over her breasts and back that he was loving her actions. Her lover had brought her so much pleasure, she intended to return the favor. Feeling his hands knot in her hair, she wasn't surprised to feel him taking over their love play. He was getting rougher and faster with his thrusts, so she knew he was close to his own orgasm.

With one final thrust of his hips, Aleksandr growled loudly as the hot, sticky liquid shot from the tip of his cock down Sophia's throat. Sweat dripped off his body as his hips and stomach convulsed and the orgasm tore through him. He watched Sophia suck every bit from his softening cock as it pulsed and throbbed in her mouth. Hearing her release the head with a loud pop, he pulled her up onto his lap. Cradling the woman in his arms, Aleksandr stroked the silky strands of her hair before he lifted her chin and kissed her softly on the lips.

Sophia couldn't help the feeling of vulnerability or foolishness that came over her quickly as Aleksandr intensely searched her eyes. She also could not believe that she had just slept with Aleksandr or that she had allowed him to do so without a condom. Awkwardly and suddenly feeling very shy, Sophia tried to get off his lap as she said softly, "Well... um... that was great, but I think it's time for you to go."

The blond billionaire chuckled loudly as he kept a tight grip on her and, once again, made her straddle his lap. As she began to struggle against him, Aleksandr said in a deep, masculine voice, "You're not going anywhere, Sophia, and neither am I. We have a lot of time to make up for, sweetheart, and I haven't had the opportunity to explore your beautiful body. Plus, I don't think you really want me to leave."

Ignoring his last statement, Sophia replied, "Just as long as we're clear about one thing, Aleksandr. There is no relationship between us after tonight. Having sex doesn't make us friends."

"No, it doesn't make us friends, but it does make us lovers," Aleksandr answered, tucking the fallen strands of hair behind her ear. "Personally, I don't see the harm in continuing this relationship. The damage is already done, Sophia. Everyone is going to assume that we are still involved after you tell Roman the truth. You can lie to yourself about wanting to end this, but I won't."

"Relationship?" Sophia asked with a small laugh. "This is not a relationship, Volkov. We fucked, nothing more, nothing less. Besides, continuing our sexual escapades would be a reminder of me losing everything, and I don't really want that."

"I truly am sorry about your unintentional involvement," Aleksandr said sincerely as her eyes met his. "As I said earlier, I want to extend an offer of employment to you, with Artem and his firm. I would at least like for you to think about it."

The sincerity she saw in his silver eyes touched Sophia's very soul. For the first time in her life, she wanted to crawl up inside this man and never let go. However, she was cursed when it came to men, and the last thing she wanted was to cause harm to Aleksandr. "I promise I will think about it," Sophia said softly as a smile touched his lips. "I'm just not used to people offering me things without a price. I know I have probably come across as a real bitch to you, but I've been alone for a long time and have kept myself out of any type of intentional relationship."

"Why? You're a desirable woman. Don't you get lonely?"

"Of course, I do, but it's better for both parties involved," Sophia answered honestly, her fingernail circling one male nipple. "I don't expect you to understand this, but I haven't had the best of luck with men. In fact, every man who has meant something to me has died violently. My father, my brother, my first true boyfriend. A girl can't help but think she's the cause of their deaths."

"You didn't cause their deaths, darling." Aleksandr sighed, hating the unshed tears he saw in her eyes before she had turned her head away from him. When she looked at him again, the tears were gone. "Their involvement with criminals caused their demise."

"How do you know—"

Seeing the glimmer of anger growing on Sophia's lovely face, he gripped her waist and quickly said, "Before you get all bent out of shape and get yourself into trouble again, I had a background check run on you. I know your father was Ethan Rousseau and that he was gunned down by members of the underworld. I also read that your brother tried to take over in your father's footsteps and was murdered. You can't blame yourself for what happened to them. Their choices sealed their fates, not you, pet."

Fighting back tears that threatened to fall down her pale, flawless face, Sophia opted to latch on to the outrage she felt for Aleksandr invading her privacy. "How dare you look into my past! Who the hell are you anyway? I know you are a major player in the underworld, but do you also work for the government?"

Aleksandr chuckled softly at Sophia's last question. He knew she was attempting to change the subject and pretend to be mad about the background search. He knew exactly how she felt, though. It had been Aleksandr and his brother Nikolai for so long that he, himself, had difficulty maintaining relationships, especially with women. He did like Sophia's up front, honest approach and liked the fact that she didn't use her tears to get her way. Didn't the redhead have any flaws?

He answered her question then. "I don't work for the government, darling. I told you, I'm the leader of the largest bratva in Russia. I inherited my leadership role from my father and have grown our power exponentially. But even though I don't work for the government, I do have a few high-ranking politicians in my back pocket."

Sophia had no doubt that Aleksandr was telling her the truth, and she wanted to ask him a million questions about his life but didn't. If she wasn't careful, she could easily lose her heart to this man. Aleksandr was everything she wanted and needed in her life but was too scared to have. A shiver ran through her body when his hands gripped her ass cheeks and spread them. She also felt his massive cock stirring between her legs. "Before we go any further, Aleksandr, are you involved romantically with someone back in Russia—a wife, a mistress, anyone? I don't mess around with men who are involved with other women."

"No, there is no one, but there will be soon," Aleksandr said before his lips found hers, once again, in a passionate kiss. Feeling her begin to undulate on his lap, he broke the kiss to ask, "Why do you not like kissing?"

"I don't know. Kissing just elevates the intimacy. People tend to kiss those they love or care for deeply. It's just not my thing."

"For someone who doesn't like it, you're very good at it," Aleksandr replied with a smug smile, running his tongue across her lower lip before slipping it into her mouth. He then scooped Sophia up in his arms and stood up. "You will never deny me any aspect of your body while we are intimately involved. If you ask me, I think you have too many rules for yourself. Too many rules means you aren't allowing yourself to live. We need to change that."

*Good luck trying,* Sophia thought to herself as Aleksandr carried her into the bedroom. Dropping her on the king-sized bed, she scooted back against the pillows before she watched him remove his jeans and underwear. She stared in awe at legs that were the size of tree trunks and an ass you could bounce pennies off. Aleksandr's body was sinfully delicious, and Sophia was going to take tonight to get her fill before her life changed drastically tomorrow. Spreading her legs to give him full view of her wet pussy while she toyed and plucked at her nipples, she said, "I love your body, Aleksandr. It's so big and yummy to look at. I bet you've had many lovers."

The bed dipped as Aleksandr climbed on. After he crawled up between her open legs, he covered her petite frame and positioned his cock at the entrance of her pussy. With one smooth thrust, Aleksandr fully embedded himself inside her tight core. They both moaned in unison before he circled her nipples with his tongue. Kissing a trail up her chest and neck to her ear, he said, "I've had a few, but none I've wanted more than you. Do you know how fucking good you feel? How about we just stay right here and tell the world to go fuck itself?"

"How about you just fuck me." Sophia sighed in pleasure as she wrapped her legs around his waist and her arms around his neck as he began to slowly move in and out of her warmth. She undulated and ground her hips against his as he pulled all but the tip out, only to plunge back inside of her, balls deep.

"This time, I am going to shoot my load deep inside your pussy, pet," the Russian growled as Sophia intentionally contracted her vaginal walls then released them as he plowed deeper and deeper into her womb. When he finished his words, he watched her tense slightly and saw a little uncertainty creep into her lavender eyes. Putting a large portion of his weight on her, Aleksandr kissed her passionately as he circled his hips, adding more pleasure to the act. He hid his smile in her neck when he felt the wetness from her cunt on his own groin. His little rabbit was easy to sway emotionally. "Tell me to come in you. Say 'flood my cunt, Sir.'"

"I... we..." Sophia began, feeling the pressure building in her loins as the friction of his movements rubbing her clitoris intermittently drove her mad.

"Don't defy me, pet," Aleksandr warned between clenched teeth before he nibbled on her neck and shoulders. He then changed his movements and fully embedded himself inside her as he started making deep, quick thrusts to tantalize her clitoris and G-spot simultaneously. At her ear, he growled, "I don't think you want to be punished again, because you won't like the consequences. Say 'flood my cunt, Sir.'"

Sophia buried her face into his thick, tattooed neck as he fucked her at a maddening pace. His balls slapped her perineum and the light hair on his groin rubbed her enlarged clit, which had her edging closer and closer toward another intense orgasm. She didn't want him to explode inside her because she didn't belong to him, but at the same time, she yearned for it. She had never let a man be so intimate with her before, but her feelings for Aleksandr were somehow different. Throwing caution to the wind and no longer being able to take the intensity of his thrusts, Sophia urged breathlessly, "Flood my cunt, Sir! I need it deep inside me!"

Aleksandr looked into her lavender eyes and mouthed 'good girl' before he quickly pulled out of her warmth, flipped her over on all fours, and plunged back into her cunt. Gripping her wide hips in his large hands, Aleksander fucked Sophia's much smaller frame at a frantic pace. When he heard her scream out with an intense orgasm, he reached under her to slam her back against his chest. Feeling her pussy convulse around his cock, had Aleksandr grunting and burying himself deep inside her womb as he, too, found his release. As the orgasm burned through his body, Aleksandr hugged Sophia tightly to his chest and placed kisses on her shoulder. The way she shook and rode the wave of her own spasms, prolonged his satisfaction as well. When the waves began to subside and his cock started to soften, he pulled out of her before the two collapsed in each other's arms. After a moment, he heard her softly snoring.

*I'll let her rest for a few,* he thought to himself with a smile. *She needs to be well-rested for what I have in mind.*

## Chapter 6

Aleksandr lay on his stomach, asleep in the middle of the king-sized bed with only a sheet draped across his waist. As the warm sunlight peeked through the windows of the glass balcony doors, he cracked open one eye and instinctually reached for Sophia's soft body. Feeling only a cold, crumpled sheet, Aleksandr shot up in the bed and rubbed his eyes before scanning the room. The giant Russian let out a string of profanity when he realized that he was alone in the room.

"Sophia!" he called out but frowned when he heard no response. *Where the hell could she be?* The two had only just fallen asleep two hours ago, after a long night of hot, steamy sex. He, personally, had enjoyed every minute of it and looked forward to doing it again. However, he couldn't do that if Sophia wasn't game.

At that moment, a mountain of a man entered the room and his eyes locked on Aleksandr. In a deep, raspy voice that shook the rafters, he said, "Pakhan, sorry to bother you, but trouble is brewing. We need to talk."

"Vor," Aleksandr replied as he spoke to the captain of his

security team. The man was not only the lead man in charge of his men, but a close, personal, friend. The bearded, seven-foot giant with a face full of scars had been by his side for almost twenty-five years. Aleksandr trusted Vor completely. "Where the fuck is Sophia? Is she in the other room?"

"No, the lady left an hour ago," Vor said, watching the rage light his boss' silver eyes. Aleksandr Volkov was not a man he personally would want to piss off. "Before you blow a gasket, Mikhas is shadowing her. She's in good hands."

"Thank you, Vor." Aleksandr smiled as the man threw him a fresh pair of jeans and a black t-shirt. He could always count on his brigadier without saying a word. As he got out of the bed and headed to the bathroom to wash and dress, he asked, "Now, what the hell is going on? Have we learned where Morrison is hiding?"

"No, we are still looking for the bastard, but we did receive word that the woman is in trouble. I take it you haven't seen the morning paper?"

"What the fuck do you mean Sophia is in trouble?"

"Your sexual involvement with the attorney has been leaked to the media and is now everywhere," Vor said, void of emotion, as his boss stiffened and gritted his teeth in anger to swear loudly. "We learned that Morrison leaked the information and is now looking to have the woman killed. Also learned that Morrison has declared himself Pakhan of Viktor's bratva and joined forces with Oleg Chechen."

"Son of a bitch!" Aleksandr yelled before he punched Sophia's mirror above the sink and it shattered into a million pieces. There were three big bratvas who controlled the Russian underworld and certain aspects of global business—the Volkovs, the Sergeis, and the Chechens. Aleksandr and Viktor had been close for years, but there had always been tension with Oleg Chechen. The fucker and his son, Grecoff, had attempted to take over things once, in the past, but with

Viktor and Aleksandr working together, his plans never got off the ground. He had no doubt that Oleg had helped Paul hatch his plan and saw this as an opportunity to take over the entire Russian mafia. Of course, they wanted Sophia dead, because she was the only thing standing between Aleksandr and prison. With him out of the way, they would all gun for Niko-lai. He could not and would not let either one of them die.

"What is your plan with the girl? Nikolai is already surrounded by a large team of men, even though he bitched about it."

"The woman is coming back to Russia with us as soon as Artem gets the case against me dropped. Sophia and I talked last night and she agreed to tell her partners about her involvement with me, although they probably already know. She is going to be my new mistress, and I want her surrounded with a team of men, 24/7, just like Nikolai. As for Chechen, I want a meeting with him, just the two of us as soon as we land. Make it happen for me, Vor."

"Da." Vor nodded before he asked, "You think you can trust the girl? She is the daughter and sister of criminals. Are we sure her career is not a front for illegal activities?"

"You let me handle Sophia, Vor. Understand?" Aleksandr asked in a very clipped, calm tone. "I am aware of who her father and brother were. I'll deal with her as I see fit, and I won't be questioned about it by you or anyone else."

"Da," Vor responded as he rolled his eyes, unaffected by Aleksandr's tone. It didn't sit well with Vor that his friend was acting so unusual with the woman. He loved the man like a brother and would die for him. "The girl is not my concern. You and Nikolai are."

"She is now. Her safety and welfare come before my own," Aleksandr said with a tone that told Vor he was done discussing Sophia and that he would protect her with his life. "Now get out. I need to finish getting ready. Have a car prepared and meet me in about thirty minutes. We've got shit to do, my friend."

---

Vor again nodded before he left a naked Aleksandr in the bathroom to get ready. He had seen pictures and a video of Sophia Rousseau, and although he thought she was attractive, he really didn't know what Aleksandr saw in the petite redhead. Vor was a man who liked voluptuous, plus size ladies, women who didn't break when you touched them. He would have to do a little extra investigation to see exactly who Aleksandr was dealing with. There was no way in hell Vor would allow a woman to fuck over a man he considered family. Taking out his phone, he made a call.

---

Across town, Sophia was standing in the elevator fidgeting with her hands as it made its way up to the top floor. With a loud exhale, she tried to calm her nerves and racing heart. She was nervous about meeting with Roman and admitting what had happened with Aleksandr, but to Sophia, the truth was the only way out. The American knew her career was over, but she was someone who liked to face trouble head on. *Well, that's not exactly true,* she thought to herself. *You did leave a giant, naked man asleep in your bed, and you know he is going to be pissed.* Oh well. Sophia never had to see the gorgeous Russian again and, in fact, didn't plan to. She was better off on her own and would be catching a plane for Paris tomorrow morning. No one knew it, but she owned a chateau in the countryside that had once belonged to her father. Sophia had already decided that she would fix it up and get a job in a nearby village. She had it all figured out, but why did the plan leave her with an empty hole in her chest and a nauseous feeling in the pit of her stomach? She knew exactly why, and the reason for her upset was the man she had spent the night with.

With another loud exhale, Sophia blinked back the tears that threatened to fall from her eyes. Aleksandr was a guy she was extremely attracted to and someone she could settle down with if she was the settling kind. However, she had sworn off relationships of any real significance a long time ago, and she really did feel as though she was cursed when it came to men. Already, since meeting her, Aleksandr had been accused of murder, and things could only go downhill from there. Sophia would hate to see anything else happen to him, and the thought of him getting hurt had a knot forming in her stomach. Sex with Aleksandr had been the most fantastic thing in her life, but it had been so much more than that. Sophia found Aleksandr funny and charming and the two had talked and laughed throughout the night. The Russian was all male, aggressive, and dominant, but he also had a soft, sweet, almost loving side. He had made sure that Sophia had found her pleasure multiple times throughout the night, and although she hated to admit it, she had loved kissing him. In fact, Sophia could have spent the night doing just that in his arms if Aleksandr had wanted to. Plus, there was that little thing of feeling safe in his arms. Sophia had not felt safe in the arms of a man since her father was alive. She could not, and would not, involve Aleksandr in her shit even if her gut was telling her otherwise. It was best if Sophia just went on with her life in solitude like she had for the last few years.

Hearing the ding of the elevator, Sophia took a large, deep breath and waited for the doors to open. When they did, she quickly made her way to the dark-haired secretary who sat behind the desk. Walking up to her, she said, "Morning, Cheryl. Is Roman in?"

"Yes, he is. He has actually been waiting for you to arrive

this morning," Cheryl replied, casting Sophia an 'I'm so sorry' look.

"What the hell is that look for?" Sophia asked, professionally dressed in a white chiffon sheath dress. She had seen that look on the secretary's face before when she had been in trouble with Roman over a file that was lost. "Is Roman still angry about yesterday?"

"You mean you don't know?" Cheryl asked with a confused look on her face. Picking up the newspaper on her desk, she offered it to Sophia. "Honey, have you not seen the news this morning? You and your personal life are everywhere!"

Sophia took the paper and quickly scanned its contents. She felt faint and the need to vomit as she not only read information about her connection to Aleksandr, but also information about her family and their legal issues. Dropping the paper on the desk, Sophia closed her eyes and placed a hand on her stomach. This was worse than she had even imagined! She could handle losing her job and starting over but not the whole world knowing her business.

"Louie, you okay, sweetheart?" Cheryl asked, concerned about the petite magenta-haired woman. She had always been fond of the woman and had found her to be kind. "I'm sorry. I just thought you knew when you walked in. Can I get you anything?

"No, Cheryl. It's okay. I'm fine," Sophia lied, opening her lavender eyes to look at the secretary. "I just wasn't expecting this. Um… can I go on in to see Roman?"

"Sure, but I must forewarn you, Louie. He's not happy and in a real dick type of mood."

Sophia said nothing further to Cheryl as she turned and made her way toward the doors of Roman's personal office. She tried to control the anxiety building inside her chest. Sophia still couldn't believe what the hell was in the paper.

How had they found out? The had to have dug into her past. She wasn't ashamed of her family by any means, but she knew how judgmental and mean people became once they knew the truth. Had Aleksandr and his team been the ones to spill the tea to the media? He had mentioned her father and brother last night and had admitted to looking into her past. He would be the one to benefit from their connection. Had Aleksandr sold her out like that? He had gotten what he wanted last night. Maybe he had planned this all along?

"Fuck men!" Sophia muttered to herself before she knocked on Roman's door. Hearing him saying enter, Sophia opened the doors and walked into the room. Straightening her back, she looked directly at Roman and confidently made her way toward his desk. She could see the rage in his green eyes and could feel it bouncing off him as she approached his desk. Reaching him, she said in a strong voice, "Roman, we need to talk."

Letting out a harsh, derisive laugh, Roman leaned back in his chair. In a hateful, snide voice he said, "Now you want to talk, Louie? Now! I find out late last night that you are not only fucking a key player of the Russian mafia but that you, yourself, come from a large family of international criminals. How long have you been fucking Volkov, Louie?"

"My relationship with Aleksandr is not what you are assuming it is," Sophia stated calmly, although she was anything but. "I wanted to tell you about this yesterday, but you wouldn't let me. I only met Aleksandr the other night at a club called Nona. I had no idea that he was the same Volkov we were trying to prosecute!"

"Oh, that's right! I forgot that you like to frequent BDSM clubs. BDSM clubs run by a Russian thug. Have you lost your fucking mind, Louie? How long has this shit been going on?"

"I told you, Roman. I just met Aleksandr the other night. I

had only gone to the club five or six times before meeting him there."

"Well, I owe Hallsey some money!" Roman laughed cruelly. "I thought you were gay, but, no, you're into filthy criminals!"

"Okay, let's get one thing straight right now, Roman," Sophia replied, losing her cool and not liking the direction the conversation was heading. "What I do in my free time or who I see is none of your fucking business. I'm trying to tell you the truth, but you're being a real dick about this. There is no reason for you to be mean."

"No reason to be mean?" Roman shouted, jumping to his feet. "The firm's lead attorney is fucking the guy they are trying to send to prison for murder. How could he be stabbing someone if he was fucking you? I need a detailed account of that evening, Louie, and I need it now!"

"I got to Club Nona about nine-twenty or nine-thirty and went straight back to see Andrei, the owner of the club. He was the man I was there to see. I was waiting for him to come into the room when a guy who called himself Alek came in. We messed around for about an hour before Andrei came into the room, said something in Russian, and Aleksandr left. I don't know what was said, but I did hear Viktor's name. Alek looked distraught after that and left. I didn't see him again until the deposition. That was when I learned that Alek is Aleksandr Volkov."

"How the hell did you not know Alek was Aleksandr Volkov? We included a picture of him in the file folder we gave you."

"No, you didn't. Aleksandr Volkov was the not the man in the picture!" Sophia exclaimed as she opened the file folder sitting on Roman's desk. Taking out the picture, she threw it at him. "This man is not Volkov! I don't know who the hell he is!

I would have come to you immediately if I had known the truth."

Picking up the picture, he looked at it and cursed loudly. "Son of a bitch! This is Volkov's brother Nikolai!" Roman could not believe his staff had fucked up this badly and given Louie the wrong picture, but then again, who the hell didn't know Aleksandr Volkov? Louie was smarter than this. "Regardless of this being the wrong picture, you should have known better, Louie! The media has been all over this shit!"

"Just because he is in the media, doesn't mean I watch that shit!" Sophia exclaimed. "I get you're pissed at me, Roman, and I don't anticipate retaining my employment with this firm, but it was by pure chance that I met Aleksandr the other night. I also won't deny that I was attracted to him and that we engaged in sexual acts. However, I won't stand here and let you lay all of this in my lap. I understand my actions are unethical, but the bigger issue here should be that an innocent man is being accused of a murder that he did not commit. I also have been provided information that points to another man being the suspect. His name is Paul Morrison."

Roman looked at Sophia with a mixture of surprise and rage on his face. How the hell had Louie figured out the information about Paul Morrison? Did she know that he and Paul were friends and that he had played a small role in Viktor's death? Fuck, the woman was too damn smart for her own good. Louie had either figured it out on her own, or the Russian bastard Volkov had told her the truth. Paul and Roman's relationship went back to some trouble Paul had gotten in regarding politicians and money laundering. Paul had paid Roman a shit ton of money to represent some of the politicians and get them off. Only he knew that little bit of information, but Louie complicated things greatly, and there was only one way out of the situation. Unfortunately, this meant that the best attorney in his firm had to die. Not only because she had found out about Paul, but because Roman knew if wouldn't take Louie long to figure out how corrupt he was. Paul had contacted Roman late last night and had expressed his anger and concern over Sophia. He had told Roman that if he didn't take care of the problem, then he would. Roman had assured Paul that all would be copacetic and had not really thought a woman like Louie would be involved with the likes of Volkov. He had secretly wanted the woman for years, and here she was trolling the sex clubs for thugs. Had Roman known that, he would have tried to get her in bed years ago. Maybe he could get what he wanted from Louie now and get Paul off his back at the same time.

"Roman, is something wrong?" Sophia asked, feeling suddenly uneasy. She had watched the emotions on his face go from anger to shock to something that totally creeped her out. She watched him unbutton his suit jacket and calmly come around the desk to sit on the edge. She did not like the way his eyes scanned her, and although Sophia was dressed, she suddenly felt naked. Feeling the need to distance herself from Roman, she walked around the chair to stand behind it. "Roman, how do we advance from here? Even if you had not planned on firing me, consider today my last day of employment. I would like you to know, though, that Aleksandr will not be charged with murder and that investigators look into this Morrison guy."

"How did you acquire this information on Paul Morrison, Louie?"

"I have to protect my source of information, Roman. However, I know that Paul has been in legal trouble in the past and was Viktor's son-in-law. I know the firm represented several attorneys that Paul was involved with. Considering he had a lot to gain from Viktor's death, he has motive. I haven't gone back and read through the files on the money laundering cases, but something tells me I could figure out a lot about Morrison from those."

"Oh, Louie," Roman replied with a sigh as he shook his head and looked at the floor. "You know, your ability to think outside the box is one of the reasons why I hired you. Unfortunately, it's part of the reason why our time together must come to an end."

A shiver ran down Sophia's spine when Roman's eyes met hers a moment before he walked around his desk once again. The gasp caught in her throat when he pulled out a gun and held it in his hand. She was able to keep the quiver out of her voice as she asked, "Roman, what the hell are you doing with a gun? Are you in some sort of trouble?"

"I'm not, but you are," Roman said as he cocked the gun back before aiming it at Sophia's chest.

"What the hell is wrong with you, Roman? Put the damn gun down!"

"Louie, you are too damn good at what you do, but this time you fucked up when you slept with Volkov. I was not only instructed to kill you, but I'm going to be paid a lot of money to do it. However, I don't want to see you die, at least not yet. Would you like to hear my proposition?"

"Roman…" Sophia began, unable to keep the fear from her voice as she threw up her hands and started to back away from the chair. "I don't understand what the hell is happening. Why don't you put down the gun and tell me what is going on? I don't understand who would want me dead! I've done nothing wrong!"

"You fucked the enemy, Louie, and ruined the whole damn plan!" Roman yelled, making Sophia gasp and cry out loudly.

"What plan? Dammit! What in the hell are you talking

about? You're not making any sense! I was with Aleksandr one night! I never plan on seeing him again!"

"Well, that's the first smart thing I've heard you say. Let's just hope you mean that, because whether you live or die will depend upon it," Roman replied, moving around the desk and closer to Sophia. Moving the gun to motion her toward the chair, he said, "Have a seat, Louie. Let me bring you up to speed on what's happening." When she reluctantly did as he asked, Roman continued. "You don't know this, but Paul and I happen to be friends. I have helped him out of a few legal issues in the past and have been paid handsomely for it. You have, intentionally or unintentionally, inserted yourself in the middle of a feud that has been longstanding between Volkov and Paul. You also happen to be the only thing keeping Volkov from being locked away. Your involvement is the reason Paul wants me to kill you, Louie, but I think we can work out another type of arrangement."

Sophia swallowed the huge lump of fear in her throat as Roman ran the barrel of his gun between the valley of her breasts. She blinked back the tears in her lavender eyes and her voice was shaky as she said, "What type of arrangement did you have in mind?"

"Isn't it obvious? You sleep with me like the good whore you are, and you not only live to see another day, but you also get to keep your job. Here, all along, I thought you were a good girl looking for Mr. Right, and you were whoring it up in sex clubs. I've wanted you from the first moment I saw you, Louie. Looks like I am finally going to get my chance." He then leaned down, ran his cheek against hers, and inhaled her sweet perfume. In her ear, he whispered, "I can show you things Volkov never could."

Sophia was physically sickened and disgusted at Roman's touch. She also could not believe the filth spewing from his mouth. What in the hell was happening? Her entire existence as an attorney working for a distinguished, reputable firm had been a lie. Roman was not only morally corrupt, but he had been taking bribes under the table and throwing cases. No wonder the elite and high-profiled wanted to utilize their firm. How many people were in on the corruption, she wondered? She was stunned to hear that Paul was not only friends with Roman, but that he wanted her dead because of Aleksandr. Sophia couldn't believe she was going to die simply because she met the Russian billionaire at a sex club.

"So, what's it going to be, Louie? You're an intelligent woman who potentially has a bright future with our firm," Roman said as he straightened his posture and his eyes feasted on Sophia's body. "We can seal the deal with your mouth on my cock right now."

Taking a deep, shaky breath, Sophia straightened her back indignantly and looked directly into Roman's eyes. "You can suck yourself off, Roman, because there is no way in hell I would let you touch me!"

In a fit of rage, Roman slapped Sophia across the face. When her eyes immediately came back to his and he saw no fear or tears in them, he said, "You stupid bitch! You would rather die for that Russian pig than sleep with me?"

With unwavering courage, she looked directly at the man she had once considered a mentor and friend and said, "Yes, I would. At least Aleksandr has been honest about who and what he is. You're nothing more than a lying, filthy coward who I can guarantee will get his in the end. So, if you're going to kill me, Roman, I suggest you get it over with."

"Then so be it, Louie. I really thought you were smarter than this," Roman replied, placing the barrel of the gun against her temple.

Sophia closed her eyes and said a silent prayer as Roman cocked the cool metal. The last thing she heard was the sound of a gun being fired before she passed out in the chair.

## Chapter 7

Sophia's eyes fluttered open before she jumped up and scooted back in the seat. Her hands quickly assessed her body to feel for any injuries. When she found none, she scanned her environment and realized that she was in the back of a moving car. How the hell did she end up here? The last thing she remembered was feeling the cold steel of Roman's gun against her temple and then hearing the loud gunshot. Sophia had clearly passed out from the shock of what was occurring, but something or someone must have saved her. Hearing someone clear his throat, her eyes narrowed on two massive, scary-looking men dressed in immaculate black suits. They were both staring at her with a mixture of curiosity and annoyance.

Just as Sophia opened her mouth to scream, the larger of the two men said in a deep, gruff voice, "No need to scream, little one. Have no intention of hurting you."

"Who the hell are you, and what do you plan on doing with me?" Sophia asked breathlessly, scooting even farther away from the two men.

"Name is Vor, and this is Mikhas," the giant Russian

replied, his face expressionless as he lit a cigarette. Taking a long draw, he said, "Just sit back and relax. Taking you to Volkov, following orders."

"Volkov? You mean Aleksandr?" Sophia asked, stunned, a sense of relief and hope washing over her. Feeling the tears burning her eyes, she quickly wiped at them. "You… work for him?"

"Da."

Watching Vor nod his head, Sophia closed her eyes a moment and allowed herself to breathe. Suddenly overcome with emotion, the tears slipped down her cheeks. She was safe and on her way, to see Aleksandr. He would hopefully explain to her what was going on and why Roman had wanted to kill her. Thinking of her one-time friend and mentor, she opened her eyes and was surprised to see the man named Mikhas handing her a tissue. Taking it from him, Sophia wiped at her eyes as she softly asked, "What about Roman? I heard a gunshot before I guess I passed out. Is he dead?"

"Da," Vor replied with no emotion. However, seeing Sophia wince slightly as she wiped at her cheek had Vor asking, "Is face hurting? Need doctor?"

"No," Sophia commented as she shook her head. "Roman slapped my face, but it's fine. Just a little tender."

Vor watched Sophia intently. Aleksandr would be livid that Roman had hit Sophia. No one, especially the Volkov brothers, tolerated violence toward women, let alone one so petite. Yes, the woman was beautiful, but he still did not see what Aleksandr saw in the American. He would give her credit, though. She had taken Roman's hit like a man and had not backed down from him at all. She also had not given up Aleksandr as her informant or even denied him as her lover. The woman had balls of steel, and that made Vor respect her greatly. Even now, Vor knew her face hurt, but Sophia said nothing. She had even attempted to hide her tears from them.

Sophia, clearly, was a different breed of woman who might fit in quite well with the bratva.

Unnerved by the Russian man's gaze, Sophia said, "Look, I'm not glass. You can stop staring at me." She was surprised to hear the two men look at each other and say something in their native tongue before they both chuckled. Irritated, she asked, "What the hell is so damn funny? If I'm the butt of your joke, find something else to entertain yourselves with."

"Not laughing at you, little one," Vor replied, arching a brow. What woman had ever talked to him like that? "Amazed by courage. Aren't you afraid?"

"Yes, I am," Sophia answered honestly, averting her attention from the men to outside the window. She hated admitting her fear to anyone, but Sophia wasn't one to hide what she was thinking or feeling. "But that doesn't mean I'm going to lose my mind and act a fool in front of you two. Where are you taking me, exactly?"

"To Aleksandr."

"Yeah, you said that, but where is he?" Sophia asked, thinking of the man she had left in her bed asleep this morning. When the two had finally dozed off, she had felt so safe and warm in his muscular arms. She had hated leaving him and had honestly never thought she would see him again, but clearly, fate had a different plan.

"Bring you to airport. Meet him there."

"Why would I need to meet him at the airport? Is he flying back to Russia?"

"Da."

Sophia looked directly at Vor as she began to nervously nibble on her bottom lip. Why did she need to meet Aleksandr at the airport? Did he think she had talked to Roman? How did he even know where she was? Narrowing her eyes at Vor, she asked, "How did you guys know where to find me this morning? Aleksandr was asleep when I left him in my apartment. I didn't leave a note or anything."

"Mikhas followed you. Knew you were in danger."

"Did Aleksandr tell you to follow me?" Sophia asked, feeling a mixture of anger and hurt. If he had known she was in trouble, then why had he not told her? Or even helped her himself?

"No need to. Anticipated his command. Why does that anger you?"

"Because I don't like the thought of someone creeping up behind me. If you wanted to know where I was going, you simply could have asked."

"Why not wake boss man before leaving?" Vor asked, cocking a dark brow at Sophia. Although he didn't find her attractive per se, he did like her quick wit and direct approach. He would love to watch Aleksandr dominate this one.

"I don't answer to Aleksandr," Sophia replied simply, her eyes connecting with his. The fact that Vor was amused, irritated her. "He doesn't control me. I do what I want to do. We had sex. It's not like we're in a relationship."

Vor and Mikhas looked at each other, once again, and chuckled loudly. The larger Russian then looked at Sophia and asked, "Been to Russia?"

"No, I haven't, and I don't plan on going anytime soon. Is that what Aleksandr is planning?"

"Ask him yourself," Vor replied simply as his phone rang and he pulled it out to answer.

Sophia rolled her lavender eyes at the vague response Vor gave her. Casting her eyes back out the window, she noticed the car was pulling into an airfield and heading toward a large, private jet surrounded by a team of men in black suits. Each man wore an earpiece and was toting some sort of gun. As the car stopped beside the plane, a silver, Mercedes Benz SUV pulled up as well. She was not surprised to see Aleksandr jump out of the car. However, she was surprised when he jerked her car door open and roughly pulled her out. Sophia was then crushed in his large, muscular arms before his lips found hers in a hot, passionate kiss. She immediately felt herself melting into his embrace and could not explain why she suddenly felt overwhelmed emotionally.

"Oh my god! I'm so glad you're alive!" Aleksandr sighed, breaking the kiss and lifting her body as he hugged her tighter. He had been so scared when Mikhas had told him about Roman's involvement with Paul and that the attorney had pulled a gun on Sophia and had intended to kill her. Aleksandr knew she would potentially be in danger but had only suspected Roman's relationship with Paul. The billionaire had not been able to breathe when he had gotten the call from Mikhas and had only just been able to release his fear, holding Sophia in his arms. If something had happened to her... Aleksandr could not even finish that statement. Putting Sophia back on her feet, his hands cupped her lovely porcelain face as his silver eyes intently scanned her face. "Are you hurt? Mikhas said Roman slapped you."

Sophia couldn't stop the tears that were falling down her cheeks as his hands softly and carefully roamed her face and neck. "He did, but I'm not hurt, just a little sore."

"I'm so sorry, Sophia," Aleksandr said, gently wiping away the tears. "I suspected that Roman and Paul had some sort of relationship but had no idea just how tight and corrupt they were."

"I had no idea Roman was dirty, Aleksandr, I swear!" Sophia said urgently, wanting him to know that she was not involved with anything that had happened. "Yes, I was a partner in the firm, but Roman didn't include me in the corruption. I had no idea about him and Morrison! I—"

"Shh," Aleksandr replied, cutting off her words with a kiss. "I know you were not involved in any of this. Mikhas heard the conversation between you and Roman. He heard everything that was said."

"How did he hear the conversation? It was just Roman and me in his office—"

"What was happening in the room was being recorded," Aleksandr commented, watching Sophia push herself back from him slightly and wipe at her own eyes. "I thought Paul might contact Roman, and I was right. Mikhas followed you because we anticipated that you might be in danger but not like you were."

"You used me as bait?" Sophia asked, anger and disgust evident on her lovely face, all tears and fear he saw in her lavender eyes now gone. "That's why you had me followed isn't it? You thought I was just as corrupt as Roman, didn't you?"

"I didn't use you as bait, dammit! Are you out of your fucking mind?" Aleksandr yelled back, running an agitated hand through his dirty-blond hair. "I told you why I had you followed and I'm not going to repeat myself. All of this could have been avoided if you had not snuck out of bed this morning and simply told me where the fuck you were going."

"How dare you blame me!" Sophia barked back, putting her hands on her wide hips as she stood toe to toe with Aleksander. "I don't have to answer to you, dammit! Don't get me wrong. I'm grateful that your men were there to save me. I will never be able to repay you for that, but don't you dare put this shit on me! I should have never gone to Club Nona that night or slept with you. My life has fallen apart ever since I met you."

"Well, you did, and you have, so suck it the fuck up, buttercup! Your association with me, and now Roman's death, puts a prime target on your back, and it's only a matter of time before Morrison sends someone else to kill you."

"I can protect myself, Volkov! I've been doing it my whole

life. You don't think I've been in danger before? I told you I grew up with a father who was an international criminal."

"But now you are a grown fucking woman who has a price on her head that several men have already bid on. You have no idea who in the hell you are dealing with," Aleksandr countered with a dark, calm rage through clenched teeth. The vein in his thick, corded neck pulsed as he said, "Since you have no idea what Morrison is capable of, it's up to me to keep you safe. The only way I can do that is to take you back to Russian with me."

"Now, who's out of his mind!" Sophia scoffed, her eyes meeting his. "There is no way in hell I'm going to Russia with you. I'm not some helpless female who can't figure shit out. I have a plane of my own to catch this afternoon, and I can guarantee it's not heading to Russia."

With a loud, animalistic growl, Aleksandr threw Sophia over his shoulder and slapped her on the bottom soundly. As she screamed out, he turned and stalked toward his private jet. No woman had ever talked to him the way Sophia had, and there was no fucking way he was going to let her continue her child-like tantrum. Aleksandr was livid with raw emotion and rage. He had saved Sophia's life! The least she could do was thank him, but instead, she was acting like a spoiled brat. As he ran up the stairs of the ramp, he felt her beating his broad back with her fists but was completely unaffected by it. Walking past his men, who sat on the plush chairs and couch of the living area, Aleksandr barked out an order to take off in his native tongue. Reaching his private bedroom suite, he threw open the door and tossed Sophia on the bed. Without another word, he turned and left the room.

Hearing the door lock from the outside, Sophia hopped off the bed and ran toward it. She screamed at Aleksandr, jiggled the handle, and kicked at the door before she felt the plane starting to move. Feeling like a trapped, wild animal,

Sophia kicked harder at the wood and yelled even louder. She felt the tears falling down her face as the wheels of the plane came up and it began to ascend into the air. Feeling completely defeated and knowing that she was now stuck, she let out one last scream before she ran to the bed and fell on it, face first. She buried her face into the pillow as she allowed herself to cry and release all her pent-up emotions.

Aleksandr walked over to the bar and downed the glass of vodka before plopping down in a chair and buckling his seat belt. He closed his eyes a moment as he listened to Sophia's screeching turn into what sounded like soft, muffled sobbing. He had wanted to beat her ass and then fuck the stubbornness out of her when he had walked into the bedroom but, instead, had given her time. Even now, Aleksandr fought the urge to comfort her but innately knew she wouldn't want it. He had never met a woman as frustrating and stubborn as Sophia. One minute, he wanted to beat her beautiful ass into submission, and the next, he wanted to soothe her fears. He had seen and felt the relief and gratitude rolling off her when he had pulled her into his arms. Sophia had kissed him with such gusto and had held him just as tightly as he held her. She clearly had issues with control, and if he wanted to make a relationship with the American woman work, then he would have to break her of her obstinance.

"You look troubled, Sasha," Vor said in Russian as the plane leveled and he approached his friend and leader. "Want to talk about it?"

"No, I don't," Aleksandr replied, without looking up at his brigadier. "Get Mikhas, so we can discuss business."

Vor nodded his head before he motioned for Mikhas to join them around the small table. He then prompted the stewardess over with the wave of his hand. "Bring us a bottle of Kors vodka and three glasses." When the stewardess returned, he waved her off and began pouring each man a drink. As he passed them out, Vor said, "We all need a drink. What's on your mind, boss?"

"Shit is going to hit the proverbial fan, once Morrison and the media find out that Roman is dead. At least we have the footage from his office, to ensure that Sophia is not charged with his murder. We will make sure that video is leaked to the Americans as soon as we reach Russia," Aleksandr said before downing his glass of clear liquor. Signaling to Vor to top him off again, he said, "I want eyes on Sophia 24/7. She will be a guest in my home, and I want no harm to come to her. If she walks outside, then someone had better be right by her side. We know Paul will send someone to try to kill her, and not only will he have his money, but he will have access to Chechen's fortune."

"What do we do about Oleg?" Vor asked, downing his own glass of vodka. "I suggest we kill the bastard and get it over with. He and that bastard son of his have been a pain in our asses for too long. You knew his betrayal would be inevitable, Sasha. That's why you've had spies in his bratva for the past few years now."

"Yeah, but this thing between Paul and Oleg has come out of nowhere. I know they see it as their opportunity to take Nikolai and me out, but it's not going to fucking work. If we kill Oleg, then we have to kill his son Grecoff," Aleksandr replied darkly, his eyes drifting to the bedroom cabin door. He could still hear her muffled sobbing and that didn't sit well with him. Downing his second drink, he said, "While I have no problems killing either man, I need to know what they are getting out of this deal. There must be a reason why the Chechens would be willing to risk war with Nikolai and me. We just have to figure out what that is."

"Insiders are hinting at the Chechens getting control of Viktor's fortune," Vor countered, sitting back in his chair.

"Word on the street is that Morrison has a large fortune hidden back in the States under some woman's name he used to know. He's been using it as leverage to gain new recruits," Mikhas added, as Aleksandr's silver eyes shot to him.

"Why the fuck am I just now hearing about this?" the Russian billionaire asked heatedly, glaring at his second in command.

"Sorry, Pakhan, but I got the call just minutes before your woman entered Roman's office. I already have boots on the ground, trying to find out the identity of this woman if she even exists. We all know what a fucking liar Paul is."

Vor watched Aleksandr growl and down a third glass of vodka before he cracked his tattooed neck. He also watched the man staring at the door of his cabin suite intently. Looking at Mikhas, he gestured with his blue eyes for the other man to leave. When he did as he signaled, Vor said, "Sophia is fine, Sasha. So, she is pouting. A lot has happened to her today. She just needs time to adjust."

"She needs her ass beaten," Aleksandr replied, rubbing his bearded chin as he sat back in his chair and crossed his legs at the ankle. "She's so fucking frustrating and doesn't do anything she's told! Sophia has no clue the kind of danger she's in now because of her involvement with me. Why can't she be like every other female and just be grateful I am helping her, instead of fighting me every step of the way?"

Vor chuckled as he poured himself another drink. "I don't think Sophia's your ordinary, average female. The woman has a big pair of brass balls, I can tell you that, especially standing up to Roman the way she did. Look, just give her time. It sounds like she has had to survive on her own most of her life, and as you know, that can make you rather cynical about others. I mean, I say you still beat her ass, but this one may require a unique approach."

"Since when did you start giving dating advice, Vor?" Aleksandr asked sarcastically, rolling his eyes. "I think I know how to handle one fucking woman! You can keep your comments to yourself."

Vor put up his hands in a defensive manner as he again laughed out loud. "I didn't say you couldn't handle it, Sasha! I've just never seen you get so worked up over a woman before. We did have our men scouring the streets of New York, after all, looking for her."

Aleksandr snarled and flipped off his brigadier before the massive man got up and walked away. He didn't need the reminder of Sophia disobeying him or that she was angry at him. Aleksandr planned on giving her time to adjust to things, but he couldn't shake her words from earlier. She already regretted sleeping with him, hell, even meeting him. Aleksandr hated to admit it, but that had stung.

Since meeting Sophia, she had consumed his thoughts day and night, and those thoughts had only grown since spending a full night with her. He had enjoyed every single minute of their time together last night and had assumed Sophia had, too. Aleksandr had loved the raw, unhindered passion she showed him. Sophia had been so honest with her emotions and had begged him for his touch, at least with her clothes off anyway. The woman was in her head way too fucking much. She would learn to trust him over time if she simply gave him a chance. There wasn't a woman he had not wooed and won, and his magenta-haired pigeon was not going to be the first. His eyes once again drifted to the door of his suite. He no longer heard any sounds coming from the room. Aleksandr needed to see if she was okay. Plus, the two of them had to talk. He just hoped his stubborn, submissive-in-training had calmed down and was ready to do so.

On the other side of the cabin door, Sophia sat in the middle of the bed, wiping at her moist eyes. Taking a deep breath, she looked around the room and was surprised to see two of her personal suitcases and her briefcase that contained her wallet. She could not help the smile that spread across her full lips or the warm feeling spreading across her chest. Aleksandr had clearly planned this little journey she was taking. The thought of a man like Aleksandr wanting to protect her, made her feel sensations that she had only ever felt with her father. However, that was where the similar feelings ended. Sexually, Aleksandr made her body come alive, and the thought of being in his home and in his bed, had her clit pulsing painfully. *What the hell is wrong with you?* Sophia chastised herself. A man tried to kill her this morning, and now she was the prisoner of a large Russian criminal. Not only that, but her life as she knew it was over. Sophia knew she would never be able to return to the States and that they would accuse her of Roman's death. Those last two thoughts had new tears forming in her eyes. However, tired of crying, Sophia blinked back the wetness and willed herself to think about something else.

Hearing the soft knock on the door, had her thoughts immediately returning to Aleksandr. Her small hands smoothed over her hair and face before trailing down to her white dress. Why did she get butterflies in her stomach every time the man was near? She had felt so relieved to see him when she had arrived at the airport. His big, muscular arms had felt so damn good wrapped around her body, hugging her tightly. Sophia had loved releasing her fears and uncertainty into him but had loved Aleksandr allowing her to, even more. Taking another deep breath and sighing, Sophia knew there was nothing else she could do now except fly to Russia. Staying with Aleksandr a couple days would at least give her time to figure out what she was going to do and how exactly she was going to stay safe.

Hearing the soft knock again, Sophia said softly, "Come in." Her lavender eyes then watched Aleksandr entering the cabin with a small tray of food and some coffee. His eyes were studying her very intently as he made his way across the room. Sophia could feel her heart begin to race faster and faster with each step he took toward her.

Placing the tray down on the bed in front of her, Aleksandr wiped at her flushed, puffy cheeks. As his thumb caressed her lovely face, he said, "I thought you might be getting a little hungry. I didn't know if you ate breakfast this morning. How are you feeling?"

"I'm fine," Sophia said, suddenly feeling embarrassed to have let Aleksandr see her so emotional. Avoiding his gaze, she focused on the tray. "I was just a little overwhelmed earlier is all. It's not every day someone holds a gun to your head. Sorry I had the emotional breakdown."

Lifting her chin up so her eyes touched his once again, a soft smile touched Aleksandr's lips. "You know its okay to show emotions, Sophia. No one is judging you because you cried a few tears."

"I hate crying. It's just a stupid waste of time," Sophia replied, pulling her head away from his touch. She then slid the tray across the bed toward herself as she said, "Thanks for the food. I was getting hungry. This looks like a lot of food, though. I don't think I can eat it all."

"It's for both of us, actually. I thought we could eat and talk," Aleksandr said as he sat down beside her on the bed. This woman pretended to be as tough as nails, but he knew, deep down, she was soft and loving. He knew this because he had felt and seen her vulnerability. The fact that she tried to hide it from him somehow touched his heart. As he poured the two of them each a glass of juice, he said, "I am going to ask you a question, and I need an honest answer. You said before we boarded the plane that you regret sleeping with me. Is that true?"

Unable to lie to him, Sophia softly said, "No, it's not. I was angry, and I shouldn't have said that. I enjoyed last night, maybe too much. Honestly, I wasn't really happy working with Roman anymore. Outside my job, I have no life. I was living but not really, you know. I just didn't anticipate this type of change or it happening so abruptly."

"Neither did I." Aleksandr chuckled, taking a bite of the croissant. "You mentioned catching your own plane. Where were you headed?"

"I was headed to France. My dad left me a lovely little chateau when he passed away that needs some updating. I figured I would move there and fix it up. Maybe open my own law practice," Sophia said, taking a bite of her fruit as she looked into Aleksandr's eyes. "Anyway, enough about that. Now it's my turn to ask you a question. I see you had a couple of suitcases packed for me. When did you decide to bring me home with you?"

"The first night I met you," Aleksandr responded honestly. When she gasped in surprise, he hurriedly added, "It's not what you think. I didn't plan any of this or intentionally entangle you in my shit. It wasn't until this morning that I packed your things, but I wanted to bring you home with me since I first saw you sitting naked on Andrei's bed. I'm not going to deny my attraction to you, Sophia. You are, by far, the most beautiful woman I have ever seen, and the sexual chemistry between the two of us is explosive. I want to help you, little one. I know your life has been turned completely upside down, and I do feel somewhat responsible for that."

"But you're not, Aleksandr. It was pure coincidence that we met at Nona," Sophia said, reaching out to take his hand in hers. "I don't want you blaming yourself for something neither one of us had control over."

Aleksandr brought the back of her hand to his mouth and placed a kiss on it. "How do you feel about coming to my home?"

"I don't know," Sophia answered truthfully. "How long are you anticipating that I be there?"

"Long enough for me to take care of Morrison and our little problem in New York. If you worry about being charged with Roman's murder, you have no need to. That problem will be handled the moment we land. I expect no monetary compensation from you while in my home, but I do expect that we will have sex and a lot of it. You will sleep with me in my bedroom and become my submissive."

"Are you wanting a relationship? If so, I told you I'm not good at those."

"Let's not get caught up on semantics." Aleksandr smiled, watching her body relax as she began to eat her food, the hand that he had kissed now resting on his thigh. "Let's just enjoy each other, shall we? We can get to know each other while we do so. Would it be so bad staying with me and fucking daily? You seemed to enjoy yourself last night. I know I did."

Sophia couldn't help the genuine smile that touched her lips. "No, that wouldn't be so bad. The sex was amazing, and I do find you incredibly gorgeous. I really do appreciate you helping me. I know I haven't done a good job of showing you, but it means a lot to me."

Aleksandr placed a kiss on her clothed shoulder before his lips found hers. His cock had immediately hardened when the smile had touched her mouth. The smile had transformed her lovely face and made it even more attractive. He wanted to lay her back on the bed and fuck the hell out of her, but he knew now wasn't the time. Plus, he had every intention of punishing

Sophia for her earlier dismissive and disrespectful tone, as well as for leaving his bed this morning without telling him. Aleksandr didn't feel like his submissive would respond the way he wanted her to right now, so he needed to put on the brakes. When he felt Sophia's hand moving up his thigh toward his crotch and her body melting into his, Aleksandr clenched his teeth and growled as he fought for control of his emotions. Damn, this woman really got under his skin! Needing to distance himself from her, he removed himself from the bed and stood up. The mixture of lust, desire, and confusion on her face had him reaching out to stroke her face.

"I want to be inside you, Sophia, but I don't think now is the time. Finish your meal and get some rest. It's going to be a long flight. You'll have plenty of time to show me your gratitude once we reach my home in Moscow. Now, if you'll excuse me, I have work to do. If you need anything, just let me know." Aleksandr then bent down and kissed her once more before he turned and headed toward the door.

# Chapter 8

Sophia sat in the back of the long, black Mercedes alone as she looked out the window. It was a little after seven in the morning and the plane had landed in Moscow an hour ago. Upon landing at the private airport, Aleksandr had kissed her passionately before putting her in a car with Vor. The mountain of a man had told her Aleksandr had business to attend to and he would meet her back at his compound shortly. Sophia had no idea what Aleksandr was doing, exactly, but Vor had said it had something to do with her safety. She had been unable to sleep on the plane but had spent some quality time talking to Aleksandr. She had enjoyed talking to him and had learned things about his family, his business, and his past. The man was not only handsome, but she found him to be intelligent, funny, and kind. For the first time, Sophia had felt comfortable enough to tell someone about her past as well. She could tell by the look in Aleksandr's eyes that he didn't judge her and actually empathized with her. She could also tell that the men in Aleksandr's bratva respected him greatly and considered him family. Her dirty-blond-haired Russian had made her laugh and forget about her troubles for a short time. He had also been so attentive and affectionate with her that Sophia had found herself completely relaxed in his presence. However, as the car pulled up in front of the gated entrance of Aleksandr's two-story mansion, Sophia could not help the sudden fear settling in the pit of her stomach.

The car pulled through the gates and up the drive as a light snow began to fall. Aleksandr's home was moderate and magnificent to look at. The mansion was composed of straight lines, a taupe-colored sandstone, with large windows. Along with the sandstone were huge, wooden beams that added warmth and masculinity to the place. His home had clearly been designed by an architect and fit him perfectly. It screamed strength, luxury and power, just like the man himself. The home was built to blend in beautifully with its wooded surroundings and, to the left of the house, was a serene lake that was covered with a thin sheet of ice. Aleksandr's home was one that Sophia, herself, would have purchased. As the car stopped, she found herself waiting with bated breath to see what the inside looked like. She had no doubts that it was as luxurious as the outside.

Feeling the car come to a halt, her door was immediately opened, and Vor was standing there offering his hand. A shiver ran through her body as the icy, arctic wind blew through the jeans and off the shoulder, blush colored sweatshirt she was wearing. Stepping out of the car, she pressed the warm wool trench coat closer to her body as she followed Vor up the stairs and into the wooden double doors. When the couple entered the home, she was immediately greeted with a cozy warmth and wonderful, masculine smells.

"Aleksandr's home is stunning," she said to the guard as her eyes scanned the impressive foyer with its wooden floors and spectacular artwork. "This is such a large home for one man. Is this his only home, or does he have others?"

"Has other homes but this is favorite," Vor replied, helping Sophia take off her coat before he removed his. Just to see how the woman would reply, he said, "Sasha lives alone but has frequent visitors. Has had many women stay here."

"Yeah, well, I'm sure he has," Sophia commented, rolling her eyes as she felt her heart sinking into her stomach. What the hell did she expect? Of course, Aleksandr had slept with many women. A man as rich and gorgeous as he was, would be a magnet for beautiful women. Aleksandr didn't belong to her and their arrangement was only temporary, but why did the thought of him being with another woman cause a sudden, intense pain in her chest? Looking at Vor, she asked, "Does he have any other guests here now?"

"Not sure but don't think so," Vor said, hiding the smile on his face. He could tell by the clipped, sarcastic tone of Sophia's voice that she was pissed. Maybe the woman liked Aleksandr more than she was willing to admit. "Need you to follow me. Sasha wants you taken to his bedroom. Will meet you there."

Sophia watched two men carry her suitcases into the house and disappear down a long corridor. She fell into step behind Vor as he led her through Aleksandr's immaculate home. Thinking about Aleksandr and another woman, had tears burning the back of her eyes. What if he was married or had a girlfriend? Did he have children? He had mentioned neither on the plane, but most men weren't going to tell a woman if she was the mistress. Aleksandr had mentioned her being his submissive. Most dominants had more than one. Maybe their relationship was going to be temporary because he had collared someone else. Sophia had seen collared subs in Andrei's club and that was a Dom's way of letting other men know who the woman belonged to. She was so engrossed in her thoughts that she didn't see Vor stop. When her face hit his broad, muscular back, she gasped loudly.

"You okay?" Vor asked, grabbing Sophia's upper arms to steady her.

"Sorry," Sophia offered, somewhat embarrassed at her actions. "I was deep in thought and wasn't paying attention."

"You think too much, red. Sometimes just need to feel."

"I'll keep that in mind," Sophia replied, again rolling her eyes. She didn't need advice from anyone let alone Vor. Seeing that she was in front of another double wooden door, she asked, "Where are we?"

"Sasha's bedroom," he said, unlocking the door. "He wants you to take hot bath and wait for him in bed."

Sophia said nothing in response as she walked into the massive bedroom. She was not surprised to hear the door close and lock behind her. Feeling the anxiety kicking in, Sophia chose to focus on her surroundings to try to calm herself. Aleksandr's bedroom alone was half the size of her apartment in New York and pristinely decorated. A solid sheet of double-paned, bulletproof glass, divided vertically by wooden beams, made up one entire wall while stone made up its parallel partner. A huge, California king-sized bed sat in the center of the room against the stone wall and was made up of thick white and taupe colored blankets. In the corner of the room, was a huge bathroom, completely encased in glass. *So much for privacy*, Sophia thought to herself. Aleksandr clearly like to watch his guests in all stages of undress. She would be completely exposed to this man and she felt her heart begin racing at the thought. When her eyes lit on the oversized, soaking tub, Sophia could feel her body being drawn to it. A nice, hot bath would take the edge off her nerves and that was exactly what she needed right now.

Walking into the bathroom, Sophia turned the faucet on and allowed the water to begin filling the tub. The curvy, petite redhead slowly slid off her clothes before pouring fragrant bath crystals into the water. She then eased her tired frame into the steamy, clear liquid as an audible sigh escaped her lips. Sophia loosely bundled her long hair into a bun on her head before laying it back on the headrest. She allowed the water to relax her body, but it did little to ease her mind. Being naked in Aleksandr's home, made what was happening even more real. Feeling the tears burning her tired eyes, she thought about today's crazy events. Thinking about almost dying in Roman's office, had the wetness again rolling down her face. There was so much in life Sophia had not experienced, and if Roman had been successful today, she never would have had the chance.

Closing her eyes, Sophia's thought about so many missed opportunities in her life. Since graduating high school, Sophia had been solely focused on going to law school, graduating law school, and working as an attorney. After losing her grandmother, Sophia had sworn off intimate relationships and would not allow herself to get too close to others. Her existence had been extremely lonely thus far, and she couldn't think of one person who even recognized that she was no longer around. Sophia had always known she was alone, but what occurred with Roman let her know just how much. With a loud sigh, the tears fell down her face. She was so tired of being alone. Sophia had no one in this world, other than herself, whom she could trust or go to for help. Just once, she wished she had someone to lean on, to love. Aleksandr was the first person since her grandmother who had offered to help her. She saw in his eyes that he was genuine, and despite her feigned indifference to him, Sophia could see herself falling for someone like him. However, there was no way in hell she was going to allow herself to do that. The two would have a sexual relationship, nothing more and nothing less, or so she told herself.

Sinking deeper into the water, Sophia found herself getting more and more anxious waiting for Aleksandr. What did he expect from her as his submissive? What would he want her to do? Her very short lived relationship with Andrei was the only experience she had with a man who claimed to be a dominant. She knew people who lived that type of lifestyle, but Sophia didn't really know if it was for her. She liked being a submissive sexually, but she didn't know how she felt about making it a way of life. Maybe she and Aleksandr needed to discuss the ground rules of their relationship. Sophia was game to try just about anything, but she did have limits. At first, she had not liked Aleksandr spanking her but had quickly found herself having an orgasm at his masterful hands. Even now, she hoped he incorporated the spankings again, although she wouldn't say that out loud. Since Sophia was stuck with Aleksandr for the time being, she was going to enjoy every delicious inch of his body. The chemistry between the two of them was explosive and she could not even begin to express how wonderful he had felt inside her. After almost dying today, Sophia found herself wanting to live, and she was going to kick that off by having a very lurid sexual affair with Aleksandr Volkov.

Feeling herself begin to get too comfortable in the massive stone tub, Sophia kicked the drain with her foot and grabbed a towel to wrap around herself as she stood up. Stepping out of the tub, she gasped loudly when she turned toward the glass door and saw Aleksandr standing there in just a pair of jeans and bare feet. Her vaginal walls clenched and pulsed as his lust-filled, silver eyes roamed her body. Sophia's own eyes feasted on his broad, muscular chest, with all its tattoos and scars, that tapered down to a narrow waist. This man was built like a god!

"You're supposed to be in bed," Aleksandr said in an almost animalistic growl as he approached her. Grabbing the towel Sophia had wrapped around herself, he tossed it on the floor. He then slowly stalked around her like a tiger getting ready to attack its prey. Tracing his index finger down her spine, he placed a chaste kiss on each shoulder. "Every inch of this body is going to belong to me after tonight, Sophia. Are you ready for that?"

"I-I... don't know," Sophia replied breathlessly, feeling Aleksandr's hands cupping her wide bottom and spreading it apart. She then felt him rubbing his clothed groin against her butt as he bent her over slightly. Feeling her nerves kick in suddenly, she blurted out, "I think we need ground rules, Aleksandr. I need to know what you want from me."

"I want it all," he whispered in her ear before he placed kisses along the side of her neck. A smile touched his lips when a shiver ran through her frame and her head fell back to allow him more access. His cock throbbed painfully in his pants as Sophia instinctually rubbed her ass against his groin. Kissing a trail to her ear again, he snarled, "In bed, now. I want you bent over the side of it with that delicious ass in the air."

Without looking back at Aleksandr, Sophia ran to the bed and did as he instructed. Her core dripped with excitement and her heartbeat quickened as she waited with anticipation to see what he would do next. She watched him stand directly across the bed from her as he slowly began to remove his jeans. Her mouth watered as the jeans slid down his enormous, brawny thighs and his giant, heavy virility hung between his legs. Swallowing the lump in her throat, Sophia hungrily licked her lips and let out a shaky breath. A slow, sensual smile touched his lips as he slowly began stroking his cock at a pleasing, leisurely pace.

"What are you going to do with me?" Sophia asked breathlessly, her own womanhood throbbing painfully as she clutched her thighs together. "I've never been a submissive before."

"Oh, yes, you mentioned ground rules." Aleksandr smiled,

continuing to stroke himself with long, slow movements. He could smell Sophia's arousal and knew she wanted him to take her. However, she needed to be punished for her earlier transgressions and disrespect and Aleksandr had every intention of making her suffer. He was intentionally keeping his distance, although he, himself, was suffering, because he needed to prove a point to her. Plus, he struggled with keeping his hands off Sophia when she was near him. "While you are my submissive, you will sleep with no other men. Each morning, you will write my name somewhere on your body. When we are out together, you will wear a bracelet marking you as mine. You will not deny me access to any part of your body at any time unless you are menstruating or ill. I will not wear condoms and you will remain on birth control and, lastly, you will not leave this property without my permission. Those are the rules, pet. Think you can handle them?"

"If I'm not allowed to sleep with anyone else while we are together, then neither are you," Sophia replied nervously, licking her lips as she watched Aleksandr walk around the bed toward her. As the Russian stood behind her, she had no doubts he could see her pussy dripping with need. "I also don't know if I like the thought of being told what to do and when to do it. What if I'm pissed at you? Or what if I'm uncomfortable with what you want me to do?"

"You still won't deny me your body. You can also use your safe word at any time, be it here in this bedroom or outside of it," Aleksandr replied before sliding two fingers down the crack of her bottom and into her warm, wet core. As he began moving his two fingers in and out of her, his thumb stroked her clit. He then leaned over her body and trailed kisses up her back to her ear. Aleksandr loved the catch he heard in her breathing and the way Sophia's hips began to instinctually move in rhythm with his fingers. Once at her ear, he kissed her cheek and whispered, "Those are my terms, pet. Take them or leave them."

Sophia's hands gripped the soft, luxurious comforter on his bed. An agonized moan escaped her lips when she felt Aleksandr replace his fingers with the head of his huge cock at the entrance of her pussy. The pleasure was the most intense sensation she had ever felt, as the width of him stretched her vaginal walls and he buried the full length of himself inside of her. Sophia tried to raise herself up slightly so she could begin to move him in and out of her warmth, but Aleksandr smacked her sharply on her bottom and held her back down with his large hand. "You're not playing fair, Alek, and I don't like it," Sophia whispered as she struggled and squirmed against his groin.

"Then say your safe word and I'll stop," Aleksandr growled, sweat rolling down his face and chest as he reached under Sophia to rub her clit in between his large fingers. It was killing him not to be able to begin making love to her, but the sweet, exquisite torture was also hurting Sophia. He needed her to agree to what he wanted, and fast, so he lay over her back and, again, at her ear, whispered, "Either agree to my terms, or leave here, Sophia. I'll still keep you safe, but our relationship will be strictly platonic. Make your choice."

Sophia cried out in delight when Aleksandr pulled out his cock, only to plunge balls deep back inside her. Her vaginal walls pulsed around his length as he plucked at her clitoris with his fingers. Sophia's body was on fire. There was no way in hell she wanted him to stop, and something told her he would. *Would it be so bad being Aleksandr's submissive?* she asked herself. Sophia knew the pleasure he could bring her, and innately, she knew he wouldn't hurt her. Inhaling deeply, she said in a moan, "Fine, dammit! I agree to your terms. I'll be your submissive. Now fuck me please!"

Aleksandr kissed Sophia's cheek and pulled at her earlobe with his teeth. There, he said in a deep, guttural voice, "I'll fuck you, pet, but first, you need to learn respect." Then in one swift movement, he pulled out of her, to pull her across his lap as he sat down on the side of the bed. He couldn't even begin to describe the joyful sensations he felt at knowing Sophia now belonged to him. However, as happy as Aleksandr was, he still had to punish her and show her ultimately who was in charge. Adding pressure to the small of Sophia's back with one hand, his other one came down hard on her bare bottom.

Sophia cried out in a mixture of pleasure and pain when his hand came down on her butt a second time. He knew a part of her wanted to scream her safe word and have the punishment end, but he also knew the other told her that she somewhat deserved it. She had left him this morning, asleep in her bed. She had crossed some sort of invisible line before he had thrown her over his shoulder and put her on the plane. When his hand came down a third, fourth, and fifth time, Sophia couldn't help the tears that were forming in her lavender eyes. By the time the last three hits came down on her bottom, she cried out one more time before he picked her up and cradled her in his arms.

"Look at me, Sophia," Aleksandr commanded softly as her eyes met his. He wiped the wetness from her delicate, porcelain face as he said, "You know why you were punished, da?"

"Y-yes," Sophia whispered brokenly, still feeling a sharp, stinging sensation on her bottom. As much as she disliked the spanking, he hoped she loved the way he cuddled her to his broad chest and wiped gently at her face. He had even held back when spanking her. Aleksandr had not wanted to hurt her, and she knew that.

"I want to make sure that you do," Aleksandr replied,

placing a kiss on her lips before his fingers slid between her legs and into her warmth. Feeling it growing even wetter with need, he knew the spanking had not turned her off. If anything, it had excited her more. Rubbing his nose against hers, he loved the smell of her sweet, minty breath against his mouth. "Tell me why I spanked you."

"You spanked me because I left you this morning and because of the things I said to you outside the plane. I was not being kind to you, and I know that," Sophia admitted in a barely audible voice, her pelvis moving against the fingers manipulating her clit. How could a man who was built like a solid, brick building be so soft and bring her so much pleasure?

Aleksandr responded to her words by smashing his mouth to hers in a hard, passionate kiss. Without breaking the kiss, he covered her body with his and mated their tongues. A growl came from deep in his throat when she wrapped her legs around his waist and her small hand began stroking his cock between her legs. When she placed the head of his shaft at the entrance of her pussy, Aleksandr jerked her hand from his cock and pressed it into the mattress over her head. Breaking the kiss, he roughly ordered, "No topping from the bottom, pet. You will receive your pleasure before I find mine."

Sophia cried out when his hot, hungry mouth made its way down her neck and stopped at her breasts. As he sucked on her nipples, three of his fingers slipped into her pussy and began moving in and out at a frantic pace. His tongue and teeth played with her nipples several minutes before he took his mouth even lower, toward her core. The moment his lips found her clit, her small hands gripped at the dirty-blond hair on his head. Her hips bucked against his mouth as he devoured the delicate nub and his fingers fucked her cunt. Feeling the building intensity of her orgasm, a strangled cry escaped her lips just as the tidal wave of pleasure broke and she came hard in Aleksandr's mouth.

The sensation was so intense and dominating that Sophia felt like she was floating above her body as the core of her convulsed and jerked against his gorgeous face. She sighed in luxury when Aleksandr's mouth again found hers and he slid his cock inside her.

Aleksandr grunted in pleasure when Sophia wrapped her arms around his neck and brought her tongue into play with his. He could feel her vaginal walls contracting around his length as he slowly eased himself in and out of her tight warmth. When she locked her legs around his waist, he picked up the pace and pumped his cock deeper and faster. He could feel his own orgasm building at the base of his balls as he intimately hugged Sophia's body on the large bed. A shiver ran through him when her beautiful mouth found the thick vein in his neck and began to suck on the pulse there. He also loved the way she tweaked his male nipples with one hand while the other pulled at his hair. Aleksandr felt Sophia's body tighten beneath him before she came hard around his cock again. As her pussy contracted around his dick, he felt his own orgasm tear through him as he let out a growl. He buried himself balls deep inside Sophia, as he rode the intense release and nibbled on the side of her neck. Aleksandr breathed heavily and emptied his seed inside the redhead as she lightly stroked his head and back.

When his breathing evened and his cock began to soften inside Sophia's pussy, he pulled out of her and rolled over on his back, bringing her with him. His fingers traced one, pink, pert nipple as she straddled his waist. "You know, pet. If you continue to please me like that, we may never leave this room."

A genuine smile played on her delicate face as she played with the light blond hair on his tattooed chest. "That was too awesome for words." Sophia smiled, her body still humming from the sex. "I still don't know if this submissive thing is for me or not, but you are pretty damn good as a dominant. I can see how easy it would be for you to change a woman's mind."

A deep, rich sound came from Aleksandr's chest as he laughed loudly and hugged Sophia close to his chest. Lying back on the bed, he said, "You agreed to the terms, remember? Personally, I think you make the perfect sub. I like my women feisty."

"Your women?" Sophia asked, arching a red brow. "Exactly how many women are we talking?"

"At the moment, just you, sweet one. Before you, I had a handful of women I saw on a regular basis."

"Any that you claim to love?" Sophia asked sarcastically, rolling her eyes. She could not help the feeling of sadness and disappointment settling in her chest.

"No," Aleksandr replied before he raised up and kissed her lips tenderly. He had seen the flash of emotion in her eyes before she had quickly hidden it. "I've never been in love before. Have you?"

"No, I haven't. I thought I loved my first real boyfriend but now realize it was more like infatuation."

"Do you believe in love?" Aleksandr asked, soothing back the magenta-colored hair from her porcelain face. He was surprised that Sophia was being so vulnerable with him.

"I don't know," Sophia answered honestly, pulling her eyes away from his. Aleksandr's gaze was just too intense at times. "I've never experienced it. I've told you I think it's safer for all parties involved if I keep men at arm's length. Do you believe in love?"

"I do. Like you, I haven't experienced it personally, but I have seen it between two people, and it's a beautiful thing. My parents were madly in love with each other as were Viktor and his wife. Someday, maybe it will find me. Something tells me that it will, and soon."

Suddenly feeling awkward and uncomfortable with the way the conversation was going and the way Aleksandr was looking at her, Sophia asked, "So, what's the deal with me writing your name on myself? I know your name. Why do I have to write it somewhere on my body?"

A smile touched Aleksandr's lips as his large hands massaged her perfect, porcelain breasts. "Don't worry. The marker is washable. I like knowing that you belong to me, and my name on your body is icing on the cake. Plus, I'll take great pleasure in finding your hiding spot."

Her body immediately responded to Aleksandr's words and touch as her hips instinctively began to rub against his rock-hard abdomen. She gasped when the billionaire's engorged cock began rubbing against her bare bottom. When his hands trailed down her sides to grip her ass and pull it apart, she smashed her breasts to his chest and playfully said, "Why, Mr. Volkov. I'm beginning to think your body likes its new sub."

Aleksandr kissed her lips and huskily replied, "I think you're right, pet. How about you show me how much you like it in return?"

Bowing her head in submission, Sophia said in a soft voice, "Yes, Master Alek." She then kissed his lips again before she climbed off his lap and got on all fours in front of him. Then, looking into his eyes, she motioned him to come forward with her index finger before touching the same finger to her mouth. Her mouth watered as she watched Aleksandr hungrily crawl across the bed to her. When he reached her, she took his giant cock in her hand and began licking at the head of it like a lollipop. Tasting the precum oozing from its head, she looked up at him innocently and said, "Mmm, I love the way you taste. Put it in my mouth, Master. Let me please you."

Aleksandr made an animalistic roar before he gripped Sophia's glorious, red hair in his fist and eased his cock between her lips. His blond head fell back in ecstasy and his eyes rolled back in his head when Sophia took the entire length of him in her mouth and began massaging his balls. He pulled himself out, leaving only the tip, before he pushed it deep in the back of her throat. He reached over her and slapped her lovely, plump ass, chuckling when she gasped loudly. Her mouth felt so good on his cock, and he was more than surprised at the playful side emerging in her. Sophia was making him feel emotions that were new, and he wasn't sure if he was comfortable with that. However, there was no way in hell he wanted them to especially stop at this moment. On the edge of coming between her sweet lips and wanting to be inside her, he slapped her ass soundly again and pulled his cock out of her mouth.

Jerking her up roughly, the gigantic billionaire tasted himself on her lips in a passionate kiss. With his mouth hovering above Sophia's, Aleksandr huskily whispered, "Ride my cock, pet. I want to watch you fuck me." He then leaned back against the pillows and stretched out his legs. He pulled her down, so she straddled his groin but was facing his lower legs. "Fuck, yeah!" he snarled when she fully embedded her pussy on his cock and gripped his ankles. As she started to bounce on him, he gripped her hips to aid her movements. He nearly came undone when his eyes watched her tight, pink, velvety pussy slowly easing up and down his massive dick. He wanted to lap up the liquid dripping from her cunt onto his groin. Every inch of her body was glorious!

Sophia rode Aleksandr at a leisurely pace, prolonging both their pleasure, as she gripped his legs. There was nothing small about her lover and she loved the way he made her feel. She knew she was an attractive woman, but she saw and felt how much Aleksandr desired her. Wanting to please him more, she quickened her pace. His hands latched on to her narrow waist and brought her down on his cock even faster and rougher. She also felt his hips thrusting up, so he could embed himself even deeper in her pussy. As their bodies slapped together, Sophia was unprepared for the fierce, explosive orgasm that ripped through her petite frame as she sat up on his lap and wailed.

As her whole body shuddered wildly, Aleksandr sat up, clutched her breasts in his large hands, and slammed her back against his chest as he, too, came hard inside of her. His breathing was ragged and deep as her sweet, juicy cunt milked every drop from his cock while he buried his bearded face against her back. His own body wrenched and twitched uncontrollably as he allowed the powerful wave of blinding pleasure to course through it. When the sensations began to lessen and subside, Aleksandr began placing kisses on Sophia's neck and shoulders. He was pleasantly surprised when she turned and grabbed his face in her hands before kissing his lips passionately. Without breaking the kiss, he pulled out of her warmth, turned her around and lay back on the bed. Their hands lazily roamed each other, and the two held one another and continued the kiss for several more moments. Aleksandr let out a contented sigh when Sophia broke the kiss and snuggled against his chest. Hearing her light, even breathing and knowing she was asleep, he pulled the cover up over them both and settled in himself.

## Chapter 9

Sophia flipped through her iPad as she sat at the breakfast table eating a fruit filled pastry and an omelet. Her inbox was full of emails from Hallsey, and she had already seen headlines on the internet about her alleged involvement with Roman's death and his deep-seated corruption. There was also a video of her in Roman's office that was on the front page of various websites. Closing the iPad and sliding it across the table, Sophia sighed. Spending time with Aleksandr had made her forget the crazy shit that was going on in her professional life right now. Taking a bite of her food, she wished she had not looked at her tablet. Shaking herself mentally, she tried to forget what she had read. Aleksandr was clearly taking care of her situation, based on what she read, but her life would never be the same again.

Thinking about the last two days with Aleksandr, had a smile playing on her lips. The two had spent most of that time in bed, making love or talking about each other's pasts. She had learned many interesting things about Aleksandr and was seeing what a wonderful, kind man he really was, even though he led the most ruthless bratva in Russia. Sophia was also feeling completely relaxed with her dominant lover. She had shared aspects of her family history with Aleksandr that she had never shared with anyone before. The more she had shared, the more she had felt like she was cleansing herself of some sort of poison. For the first time in her life, Sophia felt lighter and happier than she had… ever. Shaking her head, she thought about how ridiculous those feelings were, considering the turmoil in her life. However, the mountain Sophia had to climb didn't feel as large with Aleksandr by her side.

"You're being a dumbass," Sophia chastised herself out loud as she rolled her eyes. "Alek is not Romeo, and you damn sure aren't Juliet."

"Are you talking to me, madam?" the older servant asked as he poured more water into Sophia's glass.

She gasped in surprise. "Oh, you scared me!" She giggled, not seeing the man who had approached the table. "I didn't see you there. You caught me talking to myself."

"Mr. Volkov wanted me to tell you that his meeting is over and he wants you to join him in his office when you are finished eating. Should I tell him to expect you?" When Sophia nodded her head in response, the servant smiled and said, "His office is the last door down the long hallway to your right. Is there anything else I can get you right now?"

"No, thanks, I'm fine," Sophia replied with a small smile, but her attention was abruptly pulled across the room as a tall, attractive man walked in. He was almost as tall as Alek and just as muscular but slender, with black hair and a clean-shaven face. He looked like he was maybe in his late twenties and was looking at her with the same silver eyes as Aleksandr, only his were lighter, kinder, not so intense. As he approached the table where Sophia was sitting, the smile on his handsome face grew. His eyes were roaming over her comfortable attire that consisted of grey lounge pants and a long-sleeved grey V-neck. When they rested a moment on her wide hips and breasts, Sophia cleared her throat and adjusted her posture in the seat.

"Nikolai!" The servant smiled at the younger man who was also dressed casually, in a long-sleeved shirt and jeans. "Glad to see you home."

Nikolai pulled off his long, wool coat and handed it to the servant before patting him on the back. His eyes, however, watched Sophia as he said, "Nice to be home, Boris. You look well. Where is my brother, Alek?"

"In his office, as usual."

"Of course, he is. It's always work with that one. He needs to learn to relax." When Boris chuckled, he asked, "Is it too late for breakfast, Boris?"

"For you? Never, sir. What would you like?

"How about a cup of coffee and some of your wife's black bread and sausage? I always miss Svetlana's home cooking when I am away from Moscow."

"My wife will be happy to hear your kind words. Will you take your meal in Aleksandr's office?"

"No, I'll take it here," Nikolai replied as he chose the seat directly across from Sophia. When Boris walked away, he looked at her with a smile on his handsome face. Speaking in Russian, he said, "Well, well. Who do we have here? Are you my welcome home gift? I sure hope so."

Sophia's eyes touched his as she wiped her mouth demurely with the linen napkin and placed it back in her lap. "I'm sorry. I don't speak Russian. I didn't understand anything you said to me."

"An American? I wasn't expecting that," Nikolai said in English, his eyes scanning her body once again. "However, I must admit it's a nice surprise. You are one of the most beautiful women I have ever seen. As for what I said to you, I asked who you were and if you were my welcome home present. I am going to assume that you are the attorney Alek brought home."

"My name is Sophia if you must know, and I can guarantee that I'm not your gift," the redhead replied, as Nikolai arched a black brow at her. "And, yes. I'm here as Aleksandr's guest. He's helping me with a problem."

"Is that so?" Nikolai asked with a cocky smile playing on his lips. "Are you a personal or professional guest?"

"Personal, but not like you're thinking. I'm not a whore."

"I didn't say you were, my dear. You can put your claws away." Nikolai chuckled as Boris set his food down in front of him. "How did you and Zan meet, exactly? I hear it was at Club Nona."

"It's a long story, and I personally don't want to bore you with the details. However, it sounds as though you may already know. Now, if you'll excuse me," Sophia responded, rather clipped, as she put her napkin on the table and went to stand up. She was surprised when Nikolai's warm, strong hand shot out and grabbed her wrist.

"Have I pissed you off, sweet one? That was not my intention, I can assure you. My name is Nikolai, and I'm Zan's brother. He told me he would be bringing a woman back from the States, so you can see why my curiosity is piqued. You stated that your association with him is personal, and just so you know, we have shared these types of relationships in the past. I find you attractive and would like to get to know you on a personal level, as well, so let me apologize to you for anything that might have been misconstrued as offensive. Shall we start again?"

Sophia chuckled lightly as she again rolled her eyes. She couldn't believe that she had just met Nikolai, and here he was already trying to sleep with her! The man was handsome but didn't hold a candle to his brother. Plus, there was no way in hell she was going to share her body with anyone other than

Aleksandr. Placing her free hand on Nikolai's shoulder, Sophia leaned over and brought her mouth only inches from his. "We can start again, my dearest Nikolai, but only as friends. I hate to disappoint you, but I don't find you nearly as attractive as you find yourself. I'm only here for Aleksandr, and even that's temporary. Now, if you'll excuse me, I have a meeting with your brother in his office. I would hate to keep him waiting." Sophia then put a chaste kiss on his lips before she turned and headed down the hall.

A few seconds later, Sophia knocked on Aleksandr's office door before he beckoned into the room. Walking in, she was not surprised to see such an elegant, manly, modern space or the three men occupying it. There was ample lighting from the wall window, a massive desk, and an intimate, masculine sitting area. His walls were littered with fine art and shelves of books. He had already told her that he was addicted to the written word and had many first edition copies. This clearly was the space where he kept them. Aleksandr sat in the middle of the room on a couch, dressed casually in jeans and a long-sleeved navy button up shirt. Across from him, sat Vor and his personal attorney, Artem. A smile found her lips when she saw Aleksandr motioning to her from where he sat. She was not surprised to feel him pull her down on his lap or his lips on hers when she reached him. She curled her arms around his thick neck as he deepened the kiss.

Aleksandr broke the kiss to trail his lips up to her ear, where he whispered, "Where is my name today, pet?"

"Under my right breast," Sophia whispered back, her face flushing bright red, knowing the other men sat in the room and could possibly hear them.

"Let me see it," Aleksandr urged, attempting to lift her shirt. His eyes touched hers when her hands stopped his actions.

"You can see it later," Sophia replied in a more forceful

whisper as she looked back at Vor and Artem, who sat watching her as they sipped their coffee. "I'm not showing you with other men sitting here."

Aleksandr arched a light brow at her as he said in a firm, masculine voice, "You either show it to me now, or I punish you. However, I can assure you that if it's the latter, you will have an audience."

Sophia was livid and wanted to give Aleksandr a piece of her mind, but she knew if she did, he absolutely would punish her in front of Vor and Artem. The last thing she wanted was to be stripped and bent over in front of strangers. Between clenched teeth and her eyes shooting fire at Aleksandr, she said, "Fine. I'll show you." She then turned her body slightly from the men and raised her shirt. Under her black bra, sat his name in red marker.

Just to prove his point to Sophia and because he felt the need to touch her, Aleksandr slid his hand under the delicate material and began massaging her breast. Even though he knew she was angry at him, he saw the desire light her purple eyes. Nuzzling her neck, he couldn't help the smile that touched his lips. "Good girl. You'll be rewarded for your obedience later. Now, how do you show your master appreciation?"

Fighting the urge to smack the smug smile off his face, she cupped his bearded face and kissed his lips. Pulling back, she whispered softly, "Thank you, Master." Sophia then pulled down her shirt and moved off his lap. However, before she could move away from Aleksandr, he grabbed her wrist and pulled her down beside him on the leather sofa.

Sliding an arm around her shoulder and pulling her close beside him, he looked at his best friend. "Sophia, I'm sure you remember my attorney, Artem. He also happens to be my best friend. Artem, I believe you said you wanted a chance to speak with her this morning."

"Oh, yes, of course," Artem replied, trying to hide his smile. His blue eyes looked at the beautiful redhead as he put down his cup and saucer and crossed his legs. "As you know, I am aware of your current situation. Zan told me he mentioned you possibly working with me in my firm. I would like to personally extend the invitation to you. I know that Roman and his corruption had nothing to do with you and have had an opportunity to review some of your toughest cases. You're a brilliant attorney, Sophia, one I would love to work with."

"Is that so?" Sophia asked as she demurely crossed her legs. "I appreciate your kind words, but why would you think I would work for a firm that is just as corrupt as Roman? No offense to you or Aleksandr, but I have always prided myself on being an ethical attorney, and I have no plans of changing that. Given your position in Aleksandr's bratva, I imagine you have a rather colorful clientele."

"Your words do offend me, madam," Artem responded angrily. "You judge my firm without knowing anything about the man behind it. You assume one cannot be ethical and be a member of a bratva, and you are making yourself look foolish. Case in point, Zan. He is the leader of the largest bratva in Russia, but you could not find a man more honest or ethical than he is. Yes, he may be colorful, as you say, but this is a man who does not hurt others just for sport. There is an honor among thieves, and not all these men are bad. I only accept clients I know are innocent or have a valid reason for their behavior. Being in a bratva does not make you a criminal. Having spent time with Zan, I would assume you would know that."

Sophia couldn't help the guilt she was suddenly feeling. Artem was right. She was judging him and his firm too harshly. Aleksandr, clearly, wasn't a criminal, and none of the men she had encountered under him were, either. Sophia looked at Aleksandr before she placed a kiss on his lips as her hand squeezed his thigh. Looking at Artem, she sincerely said, "I'm sorry. I probably sound like a snobby, overly critical bitch, and here I am judging you unfairly when you should be the one judging me."

"All is forgiven, Sophia." Artem smiled, seeing the genuine regret in her face. "Look, if you would like, I can allow you access to our internal system. You can browse the cases at random and let me know what you think."

"I would like that. It would give me something to do while Aleksandr works. Thank you."

"You're welcome. I look forward to hearing what you think. Not to brag, but I've never lost a case. Of course, I do have a small advantage. I am the smartest guy in the room."

"Chush sobachya!" Aleksandr laughed as he cursed at Artem in Russian and flipped his best friend off. "You two assholes only wish you were as smart as me. You're both just jealous!"

"Jealous?" Vor shouted, joining in the fun as Sophia laughed. "Sasha, how many times have I saved your ass from dying? If you want to talk about brawn and brains, then give me the spotlight; the ladies always do."

Aleksandr laughed a deep, rich sound before he looked at Sophia and winked. "Don't let Vor fool you, Sophia. The only reason women give him the spotlight is because they're terrified of his big, scary ass. If they are squealing, it's not from pleasure. Besides, everyone in this room knows who the ladies really favor, and he's not here right now."

"Da, he is. Now that I'm back, I can help you boys get laid," Nikolai said as he walked into the room. "I know you three miss me while I am away, even though you try to deny it."

Aleksandr jumped up, laughing, and grabbed Nikolai by the back of his neck before he pulled the younger man in for a crushing embrace. The two held each other a moment before Aleksandr pulled back and cupped Nikolai's face in his hands. "Welcome home, brat," he said in Russian as the two men embraced again. "You've been missed. I hope you are well."

"Da, it's good to be home." Nikolai grinned, pulling back from his brother again. His eyes shot over a moment to look at Sophia, who sat watching the two men in amazement. "What about you, Zan? I see you have been busy while I was away. Care to share?"

"Don't fuck with Sophia, Nik," Aleksandr warned his brother, still speaking in Russian. "This woman belongs to me, and I have no intention of sharing her. If I get my way, she will be the new mistress of my home."

"What? Have you lost your fucking mind?" Nikolai asked, flabbergasted. When the hell had Aleksandr ever talked about committing himself to one female? The answer was obvious, never. "You've known this woman for three whole days, Zan, and you're thinking of making her your mistress? How do you know you can even trust her?"

"What I do with Sophia is my business, and I would suggest you stay out of it," Aleksandr growled between clenched teeth, standing toe to toe with his younger brother. "You let me worry about whether or not I can trust her, Nikolai. All you need to know is that she's one hundred percent legit and that you will guard her with your life. Do I make myself clear?"

Nikolai stood there glaring at his brother a moment before he broke eye contact to glance at Sophia. Aleksandr had never acted this way toward a woman before and there was something different about his demeanor that Nikolai didn't understand. His brother was protective of Sophia and even now, Aleksandr was almost shielding her with his body. Even though Sophia did not speak Russian, it was as if she had concluded that their argument was about her and moved closer to Aleksandr. "Crystal," Nikolai replied, his eyes connecting with his brother once again. "But when this one fucks you over, don't say I didn't warn you. It's your funeral, brother, not mine." Nikolai then let out a long sigh, stepped back from Aleksandr and leisurely sat in a chair parallel from Artem and Vor. The two men, who sat on the edge of their own seats, began to relax back on the sofa as Nikolai nonchalantly poured himself a cup of coffee.

Aleksandr wanted to beat his brother's ass as he stood there watching the younger man pour his coffee. Taking a step toward him, he was unprepared to feel Sophia's hand grab his. Turning his head to look at her, he heard her softly say, "Even though I can't speak your language, I know you two are fighting about me and I wish you wouldn't. I can leave the room and give you guys time to work this out—"

"You're not going anywhere, Sophia," Aleksandr replied, reaching out to stroke her lovely face. "My brother is just being an overprotective asshole who needs to learn some manners. Don't worry, you two will be best friends before it's all said and done."

"Doubt it," Sophia and Nikolai said in unison as Aleksandr chuckled and felt his tension immediately release.

Aleksandr plopped down on the sofa and immediately pulled Sophia back on his lap. His lips found hers in a hard, passionate kiss before he released her and locked her hand with his. His silver eyes told Sophia how much he wanted her at that moment, but they had to wait. He had other business to tend to.

"Vor," Aleksandr said, stroking his woman's cheek. "Since Nikolai and Sophia are finally here, let's talk some business. Update us on what is happening with Morrison."

"Well, like I mentioned to you earlier, Sasha, we found out

that the streets were correct about Morrison having a fortune back in the States. Turns out, he not only promised half of the money to the Chechens, but he also promised Grecoff the woman who is holding it."

Letting out a low whistle, Nikolai said, "Damn! How much money we talking?

"Half a billion dollars," Vor replied with a smile. "Apparently, this woman has no clue about the money or her upcoming nuptials."

"I feel sorry for her," Nikolai said, shaking his head. "Not because she doesn't know about the money, but because she has been promised to the Chechens. So, who's the woman? Is this somebody Paul has fucked in the past?"

"The woman is said to be Paul's half-sister," Aleksandr responded, rubbing his hand up and down Sophia's thigh as she intently listened. "We are trying to find out all the information we can on her. She is a little younger than you, Nikolai, and is in med school, but that is all we know so far. You know, yourself, we have done a thorough search of Paul's personal history and a half-sister has never come up. I'm guessing this woman has no idea what the hell is in store for her."

"Sounds like this mystery woman is going to need some help," Nikolai replied, taking a sip of his coffee.

"I couldn't agree more, Niki, and that's why I'm sending you to the States to do just that." Aleksandr grinned as Nikolai looked at him. "I say we intercept Morrison's plan and help this woman get what is rightfully hers. Plus, we save her in the process."

"That's quite the plan, Zan." Nikolai smiled back at his brother. "I like it. Talk about pissing Morrison off, but you realize we will piss off the Chechens in the process, too. What do we do about that?"

"I'm not worried about them, and neither should you be.

Paul will be recklessly running around, trying to figure out what to do, and Oleg may kill the son of a bitch for us. If he doesn't, Paul will search us out, I guarantee. If he can't beat us, he'll want to join us, but there is no way in hell that we are going to let that happen."

Nikolai rubbed his chin in thought as he reflected on his brother's plan. It was a brilliant idea that he had no doubts they could carry out. "So, when do I leave?"

"You and Mikhas leave in two days. In the meantime, you will work with Artem on Viktor's assets. I'm putting you in charge of his bratva, Niki, and that includes everyone in it. Think you can handle that?"

"Of course, I can," Nikolai replied, almost in shock at what Aleksandr was saying. For so long, his brother had tried to keep him out of the criminal side of their lives, even though he had begged Aleksandr countless times to let him in. Aleksandr had spent most of Nikolai's life trying to protect him, even though he could protect himself. That was one of the reasons why he loved his brother so much, but sometimes his protective nature was a pain in the ass. "I'm honored that you would even give me the opportunity. I won't let you down."

Winking at Nikolai, Aleksandr said in a confident, strong voice, "I know you won't. Now, if there is nothing else, I need a moment alone with Sophia. Niki, Artem wants you to go with him to his office and review some of Viktor's files. I would like to see all three of you at Club Carnage tonight, though. I think everyone needs to relax a little and unwind. Now get out!"

---

The men all laughed when they stood up to leave the room, as Aleksandr positioned Sophia, so she straddled his lap. Finding her mouth, he, again, kissed her lips until he heard the door close and the voices fade down the hall. However, it wasn't Aleksandr who broke the kiss, but Sophia.

"Aleksandr, wait," Sophia said breathlessly as Aleksandr nuzzled her neck. "We need to talk."

"I'm not sure if I like the tone of your voice. What's wrong?" Aleksandr asked in concern, hating the frown lines he saw around her mouth. She was thinking too much again and was clearly worried about something.

"I don't know if I like this plan of yours regarding Morrison. It sounds dangerous."

"You have nothing to worry about," Aleksandr said, cupping her face in his large hands. "Nothing is going to happen to you. You will be kept safe and sound behind these walls."

"I'm not worried about myself, Alek, but I am worried about you," Sophia replied softly, her eyes intently watching his. "You said Paul is going to be reckless and on the run, and then there is this Chechen family. What if they come after you? What if they hire an assassin like they did for me?"

"Listen to me, Sophia," Aleksandr said gently, touched by her concern for him and her compassion. He could see how worried she really was. It appeared that his American cared more for him than she was letting on. "Everything is going to be fine. You don't get to where I am making mistakes. I know exactly what I'm doing." Tucking her red hair behind her ear, he saw the questions in her eyes. "I see you are still not convinced, sweetheart. What's on your mind?"

"I know you can handle yourself, Alek, and I don't doubt you know what you're doing, but I think you would tell me everything was okay, even if it wasn't." Sophia sighed honestly, wanting him to understand what she was saying. She absently massaged his chest through his shirt as she said, "I just... I just don't want you to hide anything from me should things go south, okay? While I'm here with you, I want to make sure we keep things honest and open between us."

"I won't keep anything from you." Aleksandr smiled, kissing her lips softly again. "You have my word. Now, if you don't mind, I would like to discuss our plans for today."

"Our plans? What are you talking about?"

"I thought I could take you on a tour of Moscow and maybe let you do a little shopping. I don't think the few things I packed for you are going to keep you warm, especially with an early October snow. Then, tonight, I thought we could have dinner and visit Club Carnage. How does that sound?"

"That sounds wonderful!" Sophia smiled, a beautiful grin playing on her lips. "When do you want to leave?"

"You've an hour to get dressed. Make sure you wear something warm."

Sophia hopped off Aleksandr's lap excitedly as she raced to the door. She had always wanted to see Moscow, and what better way to do it than with a gorgeous, Russian billionaire. She had a feeling that today was going to be a good day after all.

## Chapter 10

Sophia walked through the luxurious, decadent restaurant as she captured the room's attention. Men and women alike wondered who she was and who she was meeting, as the waiter quietly led her to Aleksandr. She was feeling wonderful, and she looked it, too, dressed in an emerald-green, chiffon dress that stopped just below her knees and was sleeveless, with an open back. The front of the dress plunged deeply between her breasts and flowed freely below the black belt at her waist. Her magenta hair was curled and pulled back in a messy, loose bun, and she wore two-carat princess-cut diamond studs on her ears. The dress, against her soft, porcelain skin, almost gave her an ethereal, angelic glow. Her makeup was sultry and seductive, and she wore black, spiky Louboutin shoes. Sophia's heart immediately began to flutter when she found Aleksandr sitting in a private booth in front of a large window overlooking Moscow. The image of him sitting there was like an image out of a magazine, and when his eyes found her, she lost her breath.

The beautiful American watched Aleksandr immediately stand up and approach her quickly. When he reached her, he kissed her on both sides of her mouth and ran his finger down the valley of her breasts. Aleksandr looked so delicious, dressed in a charcoal gray suit with a button up soft white shirt under his jacket. She felt her core begin to pulse as his gray eyes slowly travelled up and down her body. Sophia heard Aleksandr growl deep in his throat when he grabbed her hand and spun her around so he could look at the back of her dress. She gasped loudly when his hand slid around her waist and he pulled her back against his chest. Sophia inhaled his warm vanilla, masculine scent, and allowed it to surround her as his lips grazed her long, slender neck.

"You look good enough to eat, Alek," Sophia said, keeping her voice soft and sultry, so others didn't hear. "Do you approve of my dress?"

"Honestly? I'm at a loss for words, pet. You look sublimely radiant. If everyone wasn't watching us, I would bend you over this table and show you exactly how much I enjoy this dress," Aleksandr replied gruffly at her ear, fighting to control his emotions. Sophia's beauty left him utterly speechless. "I hope you don't plan on getting any sleep tonight, little one, because we are going to be busy, both in and out of bed."

"I can't wait," Sophia replied hungrily, rubbing against his groin. She then felt him grip her hips to stop her movements and snarl a low, guttural sound. With a sexy smile on her face, she asked, "Is something wrong, Master?"

"You'll pay for that later," Aleksandr said, pulling away from her but keeping her hand in his. "Have a seat. I've already ordered us some champagne."

She giggled before she kissed him on the lips and slid into the booth. Today, had been everything she had ever dreamed of. After the meeting in Aleksandr's office this morning, the two had made love before heading out to see Moscow. Sophia had fallen in love with the city and the people she had met. Her Russian dominant had taken her to the Kremlin, Red

Square, the Cathedral, and then he had insisted they visit the city's fashion district and a couple of their most elite boutiques. He'd insisted that she buy what she wanted and had threatened her with punishment if she didn't. The dress she was wearing was one of those pieces, and it fit her like a glove. After the two had finished shopping, they had sex again in the limo before she was dropped off at his home. There, she had found a professional team of stylists who helped her prepare for an evening out with Aleksandr. The day had been so wonderful, and if Aleksandr's kiss was any indication of how things would go tonight, she was in for quite a treat.

As the waiter arrived and began pouring their champagne, Aleksandr couldn't seem to take his eyes off Sophia. "I can't get over how wonderful you look. I knew that dress would look perfect on you. Did you have a good time today?"

"I can't even put into words how wonderful today has been." Sophia smiled, cupping his bearded face with her small hand. "I don't even know when was the last time I have had this much fun. I don't think I have ever allowed myself to, actually. I was always so focused on work."

"Well, then we need to change that." Aleksandr grinned back, handing her a glass of champagne before putting his arm around her. "I could tell you enjoyed the city today. I saw it in your eyes."

"Oh my gosh! Moscow was magnificent! I loved everything about it. I think I loved watching you interact with people the most. It seemed like almost everyone knew you and wanted a moment of your time. They were so friendly to me, as well, especially since they didn't know me."

He tucked a fallen strand of red hair behind her ear before he kissed her lips. "They were friendly to you because they see what I see. You, my sweet Sophia, are just as beautiful on the inside as out. As for my relationship with them, I have helped a lot of people in the community build their businesses and get on their feet. I enjoy helping those who need it." Aleksandr didn't add that he had introduced Sophia as the new mistress of his home. He wasn't sure how she would take that bit of information, so he kept it to himself. "So, have you had the opportunity to travel much?"

"No," Sophia replied, taking a sip of her champagne. "Again, I've always wanted to but could never find the time. I figured it would be something I did once I retired. You?

"I am fortunate to have traveled around the world a couple of times, actually."

"What are some of your favorite places to visit?" Sophia asked, loving the intimate caresses and kisses he was giving her as they talked and drank champagne.

"Besides Russia?" Aleksandr winked. "I love Bolivia, Chile, Australia. I also enjoy the Faroe Islands in Denmark, but one of my most favorite places to visit is a small fishing town in Norway called Reine."

"Norway? Really? Not the answer I was anticipating. What makes it so special to you?" Sophia smiled as the waiter brought the first two courses of food.

"It's a place where Viktor took my brother and me fishing as boys. It's an archipelago nestled in this picturesque mountain range. Only about three hundred people live there, because it's located above the Artic Circle, but it's quiet and the views are stunning," Aleksandr responded, removing his arm from around her as he popped a bite of food in his mouth. "I have a small home there and visit when I need to escape the everyday bullshit. You and I will have to visit it soon. Just you, me, a bed, and a fireplace. How does that sound?"

"Incredible." Sophia smiled, leaning in to place a kiss on his neck. "I would love a big bed in front of a fireplace, but where are you going to sleep?"

"Who said anything about sleeping?" Aleksandr shot back,

his hand slipping under her dress and caressing her inner thigh. "I can assure you that there would be none of that unless it's you collapsing from exhaustion."

"You think you're that good, do you?" Sophia asked playfully, running her own small hand up his thigh toward his crotch. When her hand reached the zipper of his pants, she pulled at his ear with her teeth before she whispered, "Would Master like to show me a taste of his skills right now?"

An animalistic growl escaped Aleksandr's lips just before they crushed hers in a passionate, fiery kiss. However, before the kiss could go anywhere, he heard someone clearing their throat. Breaking the kiss, he was not expecting Oleg Chechen to be standing there. As the patriarch looked over Sophia, Aleksandr was immediately filled with rage. Instinctively, he pulled her against his side and protectively locked an arm around her. In Russian, he said, "What the fuck do you want, Chechen? You are either exceptionally brave or ignorant, to be standing this close to me right now, especially since I have several men who would take you out with just a nod of my head."

---

Ignoring Aleksandr's words, Oleg's eyes continued to stare at Sophia. "Come now, Volkov. Is that any way to treat the leader of a rival bratva? I think there has been some type of misunderstanding between the two of us," the older gentleman replied coolly, watching Sophia scoot closer to Aleksandr. Damn, the woman was gorgeous! "Who is your friend, Volkov? Is this the attorney who was working with Roman Abrams? If I had known she was this attractive, I would have insisted he not kill her."

Oleg was unprepared for the two large Russian men who flanked him on both sides and gripped his upper arms.

As Aleksandr abruptly stood up and got in Oleg's face, two of Chechen's men appeared out of nowhere. "You know who the fuck she is, Oleg, so you can stop with the fucking act!" Aleksandr barked back in Russian. It took everything in him not to beat the fuck out of the man. "Sophia has nothing to do with this, so if you value your pathetic, miserable life, you will keep her name out of your mouth. How dare you come here and insult my intelligence. You and your son are fucking with the wrong man and you know it. Call your men off, Chechen! They would be dead before they even thought about reaching for their guns."

"Pull back and wait outside," Oleg commanded softly as his men turned and walked away. He would never admit it out loud, but the younger man terrified him. Even now, Oleg tried to hide the slight quiver in his voice as he spoke to Aleksandr. "Have your men release me, Volkov. I have no intention of trying to hurt you or the woman. I would like to set up a meeting with you and your brother. My son is being misled by Morrison, and I want it to stop."

"Is that so?" Aleksandr replied calmly, feeling Sophia grab his hand in hers. He could tell she was afraid and wanted to comfort her, but first, he needed to deal with Oleg. "Then why do we have Abrams on video saying that he was working with you, your son, and Morrison? I have also seen documentation of the money trail between the three of you. Oh, and I almost forgot, being charged with Viktor's murder. We both know you fucked me over, Chechen. Why shouldn't I kill you right where you stand?"

"You wouldn't want to do that, Volkov," Oleg warned, casting his eyes down to Sophia. "What do you think the council would do if you killed me?"

"Thank me," Aleksandr said coldly as Oleg's eyes immediately shot back to him. He then looked at Vor, who stood beside the older man, and said, "Have the boys take our friend, here, to the warehouse in Garage Valley. If his men get involved, bring them too." When Oleg began to loudly, verbally protest, Aleksandr patted his chubby, sweaty face and quietly said, "Don't make a scene, Chechen. I'll kill you right where you stand. You're going to follow my boys out of here and I'll join you downstairs in just a minute. Da?"

Sophia watched Oleg's eyes widen in pure terror before he was led out by Vor and Mikhas. Although she had not understood a word of their interaction, Sophia knew it had not been positive. She had felt Aleksandr's body posture change the moment he noticed the older man. Sophia had also seen and felt the increasing fear rolling off the other man as Aleksandr spoke. Gripping his hand tightly, their eyes locked when he turned to look at her.

"Aleksandr, who the hell was that man?"

Sitting down beside her, Aleksandr cupped her face in his large hands. "That was Oleg Chechen, the leader of the bratva working with Morrison."

"What?" Sophia asked, suddenly feeling panic set up in her chest as her heart began to pound. "What did he want? What did he say?"

"It's okay, sweetheart, don't be scared," Aleksandr said softly, rubbing her cheek with his thumb. When Sophia rubbed her porcelain face against the palm of his hand, he smiled and said, "Listen, I hate to do this, but I need to cut our dinner short."

"What? Why?"

"You know why, Sophia. I wasn't expecting Chechen tonight, but I need to deal with this," he replied, watching anger light her lavender eyes as she tried to pull away from him. "Look, I'm going to take him to a warehouse I own in the city and get this over with. He was not only working with Morrison, but he was in on the plan to kill you and Viktor.

This must be dealt with, little one. Chechen has tied my hands, especially approaching me."

"No!" Sophia barked back, pulling his hands away from her face as she shook her head vigorously. "No, dammit, you don't have to deal with this now. What if it's a trap? What if he has men waiting to kill you, Alek? Why would he approach you so openly if it wasn't a trap?"

"It's not a trap," Aleksandr replied, attempting to reassure her. "I know you don't understand bratva culture, but he approached me in a public place because he knows I won't kill him here. Plus, it's a type of challenge that I can't back down from. While I deal with Chechen, Vor is going to take you to Club Carnage. I'll meet you there."

"You can take yourself to the damn club, Aleksandr! I'm not going," Sophia barked back, pushing his hands away and scooting back from him. "I can't believe you are going to put yourself in danger like this. What if something happens to you?"

"Nothing will happen to me, Sophia," Aleksandr replied through clenched teeth, her rejection of him increasing his anger. Slipping his hand around her waist, he roughly jerked her back against his chest. With his mouth hovering above hers, he asked, "Would it matter to you if it did?"

*Yes,* Sophia's heart screamed as her eyes searched his, but there was no way she was going to say it. She didn't know how it had happened, but her feelings had grown immensely for him in the last few days. Sophia felt him worming his way into her heart and she had never allowed anyone to do that before. This situation with Chechen brought her mind into laser focus about why that was such a bad idea. She had lost the most important people in her life to crime; she'd be damned if it happened again. Averting her eyes from his, she said coldly, "I don't want to see anyone get hurt."

Aleksandr scoffed loudly as he released her and stood up.

At that moment, Vor appeared out of nowhere and whispered in Aleksandr's ear. His eyes were an icy shade of gray and his tone was clipped as he said, "Vor, have some of our men take Sophia to Club Carnage and put her in the king's suite. Nikolai is meeting us there, so he can keep her company until I arrive."

Sophia fought back tears as her lover looked at her one more time and then turned abruptly to leave. Before he could walk away, she reached out and grabbed his hand. "Please be careful."

"Why? It doesn't matter to you either way, remember," Aleksandr shot back hatefully before he pulled his hand free from her grip and walked away.

Taking a deep, shaky breath, Sophia swallowed the lump in her throat as she straightened her back and grabbed her small clutch purse. She then stood up and said to Vor, "Take me back to Aleksandr's home. I'm not going to the club."

"Da, you are," Vor replied calmly as Sophia kept her back to him. "Sasha gave order not choice. Come quietly or I make scene." Just in case Sophia attempted to run, Vor placed his hand on her upper arm.

"Get your fucking hands off me," Sophia replied in a cold voice as she jerked her arm away. "I can walk by myself, you ass. Let's just get this over with."

"Lead the way, sweetheart." Vor smiled as he followed her across the restaurant and out to the waiting car.

An hour later, a large group of men led her into Club Carnage. She could not stop the fear that was building in her chest since Aleksandr had left. Was he okay? Had it all been a trap? Why did she have to fall for someone who was a criminal just like her father? She had so many questions bouncing around in her head that she didn't notice the large number of people staring at her as she walked through the club. She also didn't pay attention to the various acts of debauchery happening, either. Sophia couldn't see anything now except Aleksandr's willingness to leave her at the restaurant. She had thought he was beginning to care for her, but she was nothing more than sex. This whole situation with Chechen was a much-needed reminder that she and Aleksandr were not in a real relationship but merely one based on sex. They could be friends while he took care of her problem, but there was no future—that was clear. Sophia just had to keep that at the forefront of her mind and not allow herself to get lost in him again like she did today.

As she walked down the stairs and entered the king's suite, Sophia pushed aside her own thoughts and fears and decided to focus on her surroundings. The room was really two big rooms in one and looked like a modern-day dungeon, with cement brick walls and wide, wooden beams running horizontally along the ceiling. There was a massive, four poster bed on one side of the room and a small sitting area on the other, consisting of a black leather sectional, a large, circular, red ottoman, a stone fireplace, and a giant TV built into the wall. In the corner of the room nearest her, was the bar area where one could not only pour a drink but sit and enjoy it as well. On one wall, Sophia saw a dark wood, St. Andrew's cross beside a wide, locked cabinet that she was sure housed several BDSM toys. The room should be intimidating, but oddly, it put off a comfortable, warm feeling. She wondered how many women Aleksandr had brought to this very room and pleasured. Rolling her eyes, that thought had her scoffing loudly in disgust.

"Really, Louie! What the hell kind of thought is that?" Sophia said out loud to herself as she began walking over to the sectional. "On second thought, keep it in the forefront of your mind. It will help you stay pissed at him."

"Stay pissed at who, exactly?" Nikolai asked as he watched Sophia jump and jerk around to look at him. A smile touched his lips when she gave him an annoyed, 'fuck off' look before she sat down on the couch and began removing her high heels.

———————

Damn, this woman was spirited, but oh so honest with her feelings! Nikolai found that rather refreshing and knew his brother did as well.

"If you must know, your brother. However, I really don't need your pseudo-pity right now, nor do I want it," Sophia shot back sarcastically. "I would really just appreciate it if you stood guard outside the room. I don't plan on going anywhere."

"How about an apology and a drink? Will that work?"

Sophia looked at Nikolai and hated the sincerity she saw in eyes that mirrored Aleksandr's. Why did this guy suddenly have to touch base with his humanity? She had wanted to be angry at Nikolai, but she could see the concern etched in the lines of his handsome face. *These Volkovs don't play fair,* she thought to herself. Losing the momentum to fight with him, she let out a loud sigh before saying, "Fine. You can get me a glass of wine."

"How about something a little stronger? You look like you could use it." Nikolai smiled as he walked over to the bar area and began pouring them both a glass of Nastoiki, a flavored vodka. "I want to apologize to you for my behavior today. I was quite the bastard, and I'm sorry."

"Apology accepted," Sophia replied, rubbing her tired, sore feet as she kicked back on the couch. "Did Aleksandr tell you to apologize to me?"

"No. I haven't spoken to Zan since this morning. I have been able to learn a little more about you and realized that I judged you unfairly," Nikolai said as he carried their drinks across the room. Handing one to her, he asked, "You sure you don't want to talk about it."

Taking a sip of the raspberry flavored vodka, Sophia looked at Nikolai as she nervously nibbled on her lip. She wanted to ask him questions about Aleksandr, but how did she do it without looking like she cared too much? "I'm learning that your brother can be a real asshole sometimes. How do you deal with him when he is like that?"

Nikolai almost spit out the liquor in his mouth as he laughed at Sophia's comment. Clearing his throat, he said, "I've learned that Zan is always right, or at least he thinks he is. He has no problems admitting when he is wrong, but sometimes you just got to trust him."

"But what if you think his mistakes will put his life in danger, or worse, get him killed? How can you just go along with someone who you think is on a suicide mission?"

"Because Zan would never put himself, or more importantly those he loves, in harm's way," Nikolai replied, understanding now where her concern was stemming from. He had not talked to his brother but had been updated by Mikhas about the Oleg situation. Seeing the unshed tears in her eyes, Nikolai softened his voice. "Look, Sophia, I know you are new to the bratva lifestyle and you haven't known my brother long, but he is the smartest, most cunning man I know. He's always twelve steps ahead of his enemy. I don't expect you to understand it, but if he has done something to upset you, it was something that he had to do."

Sophia said nothing as she turned her head away from Nikolai and took another drink of her liquor. She closed her eyes a moment to stop the tears from falling as she replayed what Aleksandr had said to her. Sophia regretted, and was still regretting, not saying how she really felt before he left. Why couldn't she just say that she didn't want him to get hurt? Sophia thought she had witnessed a flash of hurt or pain in his eyes before they had iced over. She felt so confused regarding her feelings for Aleksandr. Even though Sophia hadn't known him long, he had treated her unlike any other man. She hated to admit it, but she enjoyed kissing and caressing him while they lay in each other's arms and talked. Sophia felt protected and desired and could feel herself falling for Aleksandr emotionally, which didn't make any sense. Her head told her that Aleksandr was exactly the type of man she should be running away from, but her heart said the opposite.

"I promise you, sweetheart, Zan will be fine. He will be here in a little bit and you'll be able to see for yourself," Nikolai interjected, uncomfortable with Sophia's silence. He could feel the raw emotion rolling off her, but Sophia's body language told him that she didn't want any comfort. Trying to get the American out of her head, he asked, "So, do you have family back in the States?"

Shaking her head, Sophia was glad Nikolai was changing the subject. With a half-smile, she said, "No. I'm all that's left of my family, unfortunately."

*Now I see why you have anxiety about my brother*, Nikolai thought to himself. He was a little surprised to hear that she had no one in her life. "What about a boyfriend?"

"Nope. I don't do relationships."

"Don't do relationships?" Nikolai asked with a smile on his handsome face. "What's wrong with having a relationship? Life would be very lonely if you didn't enjoy the company of another person from time to time."

This time, Sophia smiled softly before taking another sip of her vodka. "Something tells me you spend very little time alone. Do you even remember their names?"

"Of course, but you are assuming that my relationships are just sexual. Some of these women have become close personal friends of mine. What is your hang up with relationships?"

"Everyone I have ever cared about has either been killed

or has died," Sophia replied, shrugging her shoulders as she curled her legs up on the couch. "I think it's just safer for all parties involved that I stay single and unattached."

"That's a rather negative outlook on things, don't you think?" Nikolai asked, sitting back on the sofa himself as he casually crossed his legs. The more Sophia spoke, the clearer she was coming into focus. "I'm assuming you had nothing to do with their deaths, right? So why would you punish yourself for something you had nothing to do with? You're a young, vibrant, attractive woman who is penalizing herself for the crimes of others. That's very interesting, considering you're an attorney. Isn't that the sort of thing you fight against?"

---

Sophia didn't reply as she took another drink and again looked away from Nikolai. Watching the flames dancing in the fireplace, she focused on his words. Aleksandr had said the same thing to her one night while they talked. Sophia did feel as though she was punishing herself at times, but better that than hurting someone she cared about. Even if it wasn't at her hands, Sophia didn't think she could handle something happening to Aleksandr. Despite the lies she told herself, she was quickly coming to care for the Russian. However, what if Aleksandr's views of women were the same as his brother's? Aleksandr may care about the women he slept with, but the feeling of caring was light years away from love. He had already told her that he had never been in love and she believed him. Why would he lie about something like that?

"How about I get us another drink?" Nikolai asked, getting up, not wanting Sophia to shut down on him. "We can lighten this conversation, too. It's getting too deep, don't you think?"

"That would be a great idea." Sophia chuckled, glad that

Nikolai could interpret how she was feeling without words, like Aleksandr. "Another drink would be nice, too."

The two sat on the couch together, sipping their vodka, as they talked about a wide range of topics for the next hour. Sophia found that Nikolai was easy to talk to and quite kind. Although he wasn't her type, she could see what other women saw in him. Just like Aleksandr, Nikolai was intelligent, funny, and very direct. However, the more Sophia talked to Nikolai, the more she missed Aleksandr. She also couldn't help the anxiety that was growing inside her. Why the hell hadn't he at least called someone to check in? *Relax, Sophia! Nikolai clearly isn't worried, so why should you be?* Maybe the situation between Aleksandr and Oleg was taking longer than anticipated. *He is okay*, she told herself again. *Aleksandr can take care of himself.*

Sophia's heart jumped into her throat when the door to the room opened and Vor walked in. He looked at her a moment before he walked up to Nikolai and said something in his ear. The younger Volkov then chuckled lightly before he got up and headed toward the door. Before he left, he turned to Sophia to smile. "It's been a pleasure getting to know you this evening. Until we meet again." She then watched him leave the room.

"Sasha wants you naked in bed now," Vor commanded as he looked at Sophia sitting on the sectional. He was not surprised to see the woman still dressed and knew she was pissed at Aleksandr.

Rolling her eyes, Sophia slipped her shoes back on before she stood up and put her hands on her hips as she glared at Vor. "You can tell Aleksandr that if he wants me naked and in bed, then he can put me there himself! Is he here? I want to talk to him now!" Sophia's temper soared even higher when Vor laughed loudly in response to her and shook his head before leaving the room. She barely had time to think before Aleksandr walked into the room and she was immediately crushed in his arms as his mouth slammed down on hers. Sophia struggled in his arms before she broke the kiss to say, "Stop it, dammit! Let me go!"

---

Aleksandr growled as he pushed Sophia's struggling form away from him. He had thought of no one else but her after leaving the restaurant. He had hated leaving her angry, but he'd had no choice. Even after the blond billionaire had gathered vital information from Oleg before ending his life, his thoughts had been on the American redhead, but then his thoughts were on Sophia every minute of every day. What had pissed Aleksandr off most at the restaurant was Sophia's blatant refusal to say that she didn't want him to get hurt. *Maybe she doesn't really care,* he told himself as his eyes scanned her body. Could Aleksandr have misread the growing vibes that had increased dramatically between them in the last few days? He wanted a real relationship with Sophia, but he would be damned if he begged a woman to be with him.

---

Sophia couldn't read Aleksandr's eyes as he stared at her. She felt an icy, painful void form in her chest when he abruptly turned from her and headed toward the bar in the room without saying a word. Had she pushed him too far? Was he no longer interested in her? She had to find out. "Aleksandr," she began quietly, "is everything okay?"

"I thought you didn't give a fuck, remember?" Aleksandr asked sarcastically as he poured himself a glass of whiskey and downed it. As he poured the second one, he said, "I took care of the problem. That is all you need to know."

"You told me you wouldn't keep anything from me,"

Sophia replied softly as she walked toward the bar where he stood. "Is Oleg still alive?"

"No," Aleksandr said simply before he downed a second shot of whiskey.

"Did you kill him?"

His eyes locked with hers as he said coldly, "Yes, I did. Does that bother you?"

"Yeah, it does," Sophia said softly before Aleksandr scoffed loudly and threw the glass across the room, shattering it against the stone wall. As he swiftly approached her with angry strides, she put out her hands to stop him as she hurriedly said, "But not like you're thinking."

"Then fucking explain it to me, Sophia!" Aleksandr barked, hitting his chest with his fist. "I can't read your mind!"

"I'm… I'm…" Sophia tried before she let out a sigh of exasperation. "I'm sorry, Aleksandr! Okay? I'm sorry, dammit! I was worried about you. I should have said so back at the restaurant, but I was pissed at you. You left me with absolutely no explanation of what in the hell you were doing or where you were going or even what was happening. You know I don't speak Russian, yet you had a full conversation with Oleg before bouncing out of the place to go kill him. I was scared, you jerk, and you didn't give a damn. I understand you have a specific role to play, being the leader of a bratva and all, but next time, a heads up would be appreciated."

Aleksandr stood there in stunned silence as Sophia's words sunk in. He couldn't help the smile that spread across his face as he stood there staring at her. Sophia did care about him, and here she was, confessing it to him. Only his American could make an apology sound like an argument. Walking up to her, he cupped her face before placing a soft kiss on her lips. Pulling back, his thumb stroked her cheek gently. "I wish you would have said this before I left the restaurant, but I guess I can accept your apology now." Aleksandr smiled as Sophia crossed her arms over her chest and opened her mouth to speak again. Before she could say anything, he passionately kissed her mouth and brought his tongue into play. With his lips against hers, he said, "I'm sorry too, Sophia. I should have told you what was happening. I can see why you were angry at me."

Sophia slammed her lips against Aleksandr's as her hands began pulling off his suit jacket. Once it was off, she quickly tore off his tie and unbuttoned his shirt while his large hands roamed her body and his lips devoured her face and neck. When the upper half of him was naked and his muscular, tattooed chest was exposed to her, she ran her hands over the soft blond hair there and backed up slowly. As Aleksandr watched, the beautiful redhead gently removed her dress and undergarments until she stood before him in only her black, spiky heels. She then knelt on her knees in front of him and bowed her head. Without looking up at him, she softly asked, "What does Master want to do with his pet this evening?"

Aleksandr's grey eyes darkened with lust as his hand began to massage his rock-hard cock through his pants. As he slowly approached her, Aleksandr removed his thick, throbbing rod and began to stroke it with long, unhurried movements. With his free hand, he raised her chin with his finger. When her eyes met his, Aleksandr had a sexy grin on his handsome face. "There are so many things I plan on doing to you tonight, pet, but first, I want you lying in the middle of the bed with your legs spread wide."

Sophia's hand shot up to wrap around his cock before she lovingly rubbed it across her lips. Running her tongue along the slit in the head, she tasted the salty precum. Her voice was soft and sultry as she looked up at him and smiled. "But I want to taste you first."

"You will in time, but right now, I want to please you," Aleksandr replied with a grin, taking her hand off his dick and helping her stand up. He then rubbed the head of his cock against the engorged clit peeking out of her vaginal lips as he kissed her mouth. "There will be plenty of time for you to suck me off later, I promise. Now get in bed. I can't wait much longer."

Sophia ran to the bed and quickly did as he asked. As she lay back on the mound of pillows, her hungry eyes watched her lover walk over to the large closet by the St. Andrew's cross and open it. He pulled out four colorful silk strands, a curved, vibrating butt plug, and some lubricant. As he walked toward the bed with the items, Sophia sat up and began to nibble on her lips nervously. She had never done any type of anal play before and had no idea what he was going to do with the silk. "What are you going to do with those things?" she asked as he laid them on the bed beside her.

"We're going to experiment." Aleksandr winked before he pulled off his pants and covered her body with his. Then before she could respond, the gorgeous blond eased his cock into her tight, wet warmth as they both sighed in ecstasy. He began nibbling on her neck as he braced himself above her and slowly began to move himself in and out of her. At her ear, he huskily whispered, "I'm going to play with that delicious ass tonight and you are going to let me, but first, I need to get you comfortable. If at any time, you want to stop, just say your safe word."

Sophia responded by hungrily kissing his lips and wrapping her legs around his waist as he rode her. Although she was nervous about the anal play, she knew she would let Aleksandr do whatever he wanted because she trusted him. When he broke the kiss and tried to pull out of her, she dug her heels into his muscular ass and began to devour his neck. She hid the giggle that dared to escape her lips when an animalistic growl of euphoria fell from his mouth. Sophia whispered, "Don't pull out yet, baby. I need to come."

Aleksandr stilled his movements as he raised his head and looked at her flawless face. Cocking a brow at her, he asked, "Are we topping from the bottom again, pet? I must not be doing a good job of showing you who is in charge. How about we change that?" Aleksandr then abruptly pulled his cock out and slapped the mound of her pussy with his thick, heavy shaft. He then flipped her over and painfully brought his massive hand down against one porcelain cheek before he moved away from her and began tying her hands and legs to the posts of the bed. When she began to verbally protest and struggle against the silks, he smacked her ass once more. "Stop moving, or I'll paint that alabaster skin red."

Sophia immediately stopped struggling and moving as Aleksandr finished tightening the silks. She then felt him reach under her before hauling her ass up in the air. Sophia moaned loudly when his hot mouth began trailing a path down her spine toward her bottom and jerked slightly when he began nibbling on one pale cheek. An agonized cry escaped her lips when his tongue found her dripping wet core and began suckling on her clit. As he licked and pulled at the nub with his teeth, Sophia squirmed her core against his hungry mouth. Her pussy dripped down her inner thighs as she felt the orgasm building deep within. Sophia's hips began to instinctively rock back and forth against his fingers when he slid three of them in the entrance of her core. Within seconds, she felt the scream escape her throat as she came hard inside Aleksandr's mouth.

He drank every bit of her essence as the orgasm tore through her body. He loved the purrs and soft moans coming from her lips as she rode the wave of pleasure. When the orgasm began to subside, Aleksandr pulled out his fingers and placed a kiss on both of her cheeks. He then picked up the lubricant and vibrating butt plug and began to prepare it. As he did, he said in a stern, commanding voice, "I need you to relax, pet. This may be uncomfortable at first, but you'll like it. I promise."

Sophia took a deep breath and told herself to relax as she felt Aleksandr moving behind her. When his hand began spreading her cheeks apart, she couldn't help but tighten her muscles. He clearly anticipated her actions because she then felt him begin to circle her clit with his free hand in slow, delicious movements. Her pussy once again began to ooze with her own warm liquid before the curved butt plug was pushed into her anus. She let out a loud gasp of discomfort, then the feeling began to immediately lessen when the small, pulsing vibrations began. The sensations coming from the butt plug were also stimulating her clitoris due to a piece that extended from her anus to the sensitive nub. The irritation and soreness were soon replaced with a building intensity in the pit of her stomach. She hated to admit it but, damn, it felt good.

Lying beside Sophia on the bed, Aleksandr kicked the vibrations up a notch as he brushed the fallen red hair away from her face. He loved watching her pull against the restraints and the rapture he saw in her eyes. Reaching under his woman, he plucked at her blush-colored nipples. Placing a kiss on her cheek, he asked in a husky, deep voice, "Do you know how beautiful you look right now, Sophia? I love every inch of this tantalizing body and have no intention of ever letting you go. Tell me you belong to me, pet. Tell me you will never leave me."

Sophia swallowed the lump in her throat as she listened to Aleksandr's words. His eyes were so sincere, and her heart screamed at her to repeat his words. When she didn't answer right away, he kicked up the vibrations in her lower half. She tried clenching her thighs together but was unable to do so. Bucking her hips, Sophia buried her face in her bicep. "I belong to you, Master," she responded breathlessly, averting Aleksandr's gaze.

"Not good enough, pet," the Russian billionaire replied as he kicked the vibrations up again before he gripped her red hair in his free hand and jerked her head so she could look him directly in his eyes. Running his tongue across her luscious lips, he repeated his earlier command, "Tell me you will never leave me." When she, again, avoided his gaze by closing her eyes, Aleksandr growled loudly before he released her hair and sat up on the bed. The blond giant then positioned himself between her open thighs as he eased the head of his cock into the entrance of her perfect, wet pussy. As he did this, he notched the vibrations up once more before his hand came down hard on her bottom. Sophia cried out in a mixture of pleasure and pain when it came down a third and fourth time. "If you want the punishment to stop, pet, then tell me what I want to hear."

Sophia felt the tears burning her eyes as his hand struck her a sixth and seventh time. Her body was on overload. Between Aleksandr's spanking, the vibrations from the toy, and his thick, mouth-watering cock fucking her, she didn't know how much more she could stand. When he slapped her painfully a ninth time, Sophia screamed out, "I'll never leave you, Master. I swear!"

Embedding his cock balls deep inside her, Aleksandr leaned over and placed gentle kisses on her pale shoulders. He couldn't help the shit-eating grin that spread across his face as he said, "Good girl. That's right; you'll never leave me. You will always belong to me. We'll work on how much you love me later." When Sophia gasped in shock, Aleksandr raised up, gripped her hips, and began riding his American with a frenzied fever. He felt and heard Sophia's immediate orgasm and she screamed at the top of her lungs as her vaginal walls convulsed around his cock. Her juices exploded around him and poured down his thighs as he fucked her at a maddening pace. He kicked the vibrations up on the toy, to prolong her sensations, as sweat poured off his chest onto her back. Then with one final push, Aleksandr yelled out in total and complete satisfaction. He buried his cock inside Sophia as deep as he could as his semen shot from him like a volatile blast deep into her core. His own body convulsed and jerked in rhythm to Sophia's as the second intense orgasm coursed through her body again. They each rode the enormous, powerful wave until it began to trough.

Needing to feel Sophia in his arms, Aleksandr removed his softening member from her warmth as a shiver of delight ran through his massive body. He quickly took out the toy and untied the restraints before he lay back on the pillows and pulled her limp, tired body up on his chest. A smile touched his lips when she wrapped her arms around him, snuggled closer, and began placing butterfly kisses on his chest. He placed a kiss on her head and let out a contented sigh. "Damn, woman, you wear me out."

"I wear *you* out?" Sophia asked, resting her head on his muscular, tattooed chest as she looked up at him. "I do believe you instigated this whole encounter, Sir."

"*I* instigated? Who took off her clothes and got into submissive position?" Aleksandr teased, bending his head to kiss her lips playfully. "I do believe that was you. Did you like the anal play?"

"I can't believe I'm saying this, but I did."

"Just wait until my cock replaces the plug." Aleksandr smiled, raising his eyebrows up and down comically. "It will feel even better."

"We'll see about that," Sophia replied with a smile of her own before she placed another kiss on his chest and played with the light blond hair there. Her thoughts went to the comment Aleksandr had made about her loving him, as the two fell into a comfortable silence. The thought of loving her dominant made a sweet, delightful warmth spread across her chest and a smile touch her lips. Could she fall in love with Aleksandr? She was afraid that she already had.

"You're awfully quiet, love. What are you thinking about?" Aleksandr asked, wanting the moment between the two of them to never end. He had been intimate with many women in his past, but for the first time in his life, he found himself only wanting one. Aleksandr had wanted to hear Sophia say that she loved him but knew the redhead wasn't ready for that.

"Nothing, really. Just how nice today was," Sophia lied, wanting to avoid any conversations associated with love. Resting her chin on his chest, her eyes found his. "I really am sorry about earlier. Of course, it would bother me if something happened to you. I was just being immature and cruel. Did everything really go okay with Oleg tonight?"

"All is forgiven," Aleksandr answered honestly, running his fingertips up and down her bare back. Her skin was petal soft. "As for Oleg, he's dead, Sophia. I won't go into the details of how with you, but I was able to obtain some vital information from him about Morrison before he died."

"What type of information did you get?"

"Well, for starters, I know where the worthless bastard is hiding out. I also know the identity of his half-sister in the States. He, unfortunately, wouldn't give me any information on his son. I'm not surprised, though."

"Are you worried the council will retaliate against you for killing Oleg?" Sophia asked, concern etched all over her face as she fingered his bearded jaw.

"No, I'm not, and neither should you be," Aleksandr said before kissing her lips softly. "The council knows I've tolerated Oleg for years now. However, once they hear of how he approached me tonight, they will understand and accept my actions. Although you won't understand this, me killing Chechen solidifies me as the first choice to lead the council."

"I'm assuming since you know where Paul is that you will be going after him?"

"Yes," Aleksandr responded honestly before he rolled Sophia underneath him in one swift movement. He could feel his cock begin to harden between her legs as he lovingly kissed her lips. When she ran her foot down his thigh and calf, he easily slid himself inside her tight pussy. As they both sighed in satisfaction, he braced himself on one arm and explored her lovely face with his silver eyes. "Now, no more talk of Chechen tonight. We'll talk about that in the morning. Right now, all I want is you."

"I'm yours for the taking, baby. Do what you want with me." Sophia smiled, running her hands up and down his back as he began to move himself inside her. She still had many questions and was scared about what could potentially happen to Aleksandr, but right now, she wanted to enjoy her time with him. The two then proceeded to make love until the wee hours of the morning and do just that.

## Chapter 11

Sophia lay on the cozy, light grey couch, wrapped in a faux rabbit fur throw as she read through one of the case files from Artem's law firm. The room was modern, luxurious, and cozy and was one of two living rooms Aleksandr had in his home. It had two walls of insulated windows and a fireplace that spanned the width of a third wall. She looked up from the laptop a moment to watch the snow falling outside. She sighed happily as she thought about the last two weeks with Aleksandr. Her days had been spent going over cases and consulting with Artem, and her nights had been spent making love and simply enjoying Aleksandr's company. She glanced down at the platinum and diamond cluster tennis bracelet he had given her after their amazing night of sex at Club Carnage. Sophia had initially refused the gift, but Aleksandr had insisted she take it and wear it, as his submissive. Although she had thanked Aleksandr many times for the gift in and out of the bedroom, it had meant more to her than Sophia even cared to admit. It was the first time she had received a gift from a man since her father was alive. She had been able to hide the tears from Aleksandr but had let them flow once he had gone to sleep.

Sitting up on the couch, Sophia picked up the glass of wine from the mirrored coffee table. After taking a drink, Sophia went back to snacking on the bruschetta covered in ricotta cheese and strawberries that Boris had brought her. Aleksandr was taking her out for dinner tonight and she didn't want to ruin it by eating a large lunch. Her lover was at work and had mentioned a conference call with Nikolai, who was in the States trying to acquire some woman named Piper who was being hunted by Paul Morrison and Grecoff Chechen. The two men had, of course, been on the run since Aleksandr had killed Oleg. Her lover had met with Vor and his men several times over the past couple of weeks about how to handle both men, but he was having trouble finding them. Not only did the billionaire have that on his plate, but he was being pressured to take over the bratva council. Aleksandr had voiced to her that he didn't want to take control of the whole underworld, but he really wasn't being given much of a choice. Not only was he not being given a choice, but his father had held the title for several years and Aleksandr felt it was somehow his legacy to take the position.

Sighing loudly, Sophia took another drink of her wine. She really felt like she was stuck between a rock and a hard place. Sophia had fallen in love with Aleksandr and she was finally willing to admit it to herself, although she was not ready to tell him. Part of her didn't want Aleksandr finding Paul because, once he did, she would have no excuse to stay with him. Right now, she could use her situation to hide her true feelings, but when Aleksandr caught Paul, she would be forced to either tell him the truth or walk away from him. The thought of walking away made her chest ache painfully and her stomach violently ill. What made things worse was she had no idea how Aleksandr felt about her, either, because her lover had been very tight-lipped. Sophia knew he enjoyed her company and her body, but did his emotions go beyond that? She had caught him simply watching her several times and she would have sworn that her feelings were mirrored in his beautiful, silver eyes, but what if she was wrong? Sophia knew what would happen; she would be utterly and completely devastated.

Wiping the tears that threatened to fall, she pushed away all the negative thoughts and lay back down on the sofa. She resumed reading the notes on a high-profile case that Artem had just prosecuted. The lawyer was brilliant and very strategic in his work. The more files she reviewed, the more she could see herself working with the man. Artem had already told her that if she chose to stay in Moscow and decided to work with him, he would rename his firm to include her. Sophia found herself growing a friendship with Artem and liked the friendly sparring they did over cases. It also touched her to see how much Artem cared for Aleksandr and his brother Nikolai. The men were family and treated each other with love and respect. Sophia only hoped to one day be a part of something like that. *Get your head out of the clouds,* she chastised herself. *You don't even know how the hell Aleksandr feels about you, and here you are planning a family.*

Sophia was so lost in her own thoughts that she didn't hear Aleksandr enter the room. She gasped when she felt his large hand run up the back of her thigh and lovingly pat her bottom. She turned her head to look up at him, but she was roughly pulled up in his arms and across his lap to straddle. She moaned in pleasure when he found her mouth and his hands slid up under the pink hoodie she wore. She let out a shriek and jerked back from her lover when his icy hands connected with her sides. "Stop, dammit! Your hands are cold!"

Aleksandr chuckled loudly as he removed his hands from under her shirt and hugged her to his chest. "Did you miss me today, sweetheart? I missed you."

"I might have," Sophia replied with a smile, kissing his lips as she played with the hair at the nape of his thick neck. "How was work today?"

"Stressful, but I have to say that coming home to you has made things better," Aleksandr said, enjoying the feel of Sophia on his lap. He could already feel his semi-hard cock beginning to react to her. It amazed him how quickly his body reacted to Sophia being near him. She plagued his thoughts every minute of every day, and today was no exception. Leaning into her, he thought about the events of the day and how they had unfolded. Needing to lose himself in her, he nuzzled his bearded face against her neck. "I see you have on my bracelet. Where is my name today?"

"On my left butt cheek," Sophia said, loving the feel of his arms around her. "Would you like to see it, Master?"

"Absolutely, pet, but first, we need to talk," Aleksandr softly replied as Sophia pushed back against his chest and their eyes met. He hated the concern and worry he saw leap into her eyes as he stroked her cheek. He also knew that she was not going to like what he had to say, but she had to know the truth.

"What's wrong, Aleksandr?" Sophia asked in concern, cupping the sides of his face lovingly. "I can see in your eyes that something is wrong. Is Nikolai okay? Did you talk to him today?"

"I did, and that is what we need to talk about." Aleksandr sighed, gripping Sophia's hips to keep her still as she tried to move off his lap. When she stopped struggling, he said, "We found Paul, Sophia. We know exactly where the bastard is."

"You did?" she questioned in surprise. "Where is he?"

"He's in the States, Las Vegas, actually. One of our men spotted him and Chechen together last night. We were able to have them followed, and they have a plan to not only go after his half-sister but to kill Nikolai as well. Lucky for us, we gained access to this plan and have come up with a way to intercept it."

"Intercept?" Sophia asked, confusion evident on her beautiful porcelain face. "How can you do that from all the way in Moscow?"

"I won't be in Moscow, Sophia. I'm flying to Las Vegas tonight."

"No!" Sophia replied sharply, shaking her head as she gripped his suit jacket. "No, dammit! Can't you send someone else to kill Paul? Why do you personally have to fly to Vegas? Maybe we can just leave Paul be? I mean, he hasn't tried to bother me since I came to Moscow, so maybe he's changed his mind about killing me. I'm sure you intimidate the hell out of him."

Aleksandr cast his eyes down a moment and sighed loudly. "Morrison has actually tried twice to get to you, Sophia," the blond giant began hesitantly, raising his head to look at her again as guilt burned his stomach. He had not wanted to tell Sophia about the attempts on her life because he had not wanted to scare her, but he could tell what a mistake that was by the hurt evident in her eyes. Seeing the questions on her face, he said, "The first time was very shortly after you arrived here. He hired another assassin, who tried to break in and kill you. Mikhas caught him and killed him instantly."

"And the other time?" Sophia asked in a voice barely an audible whisper.

"About a week ago, there was a woman posing as our maid, Daria. Come to find out, this woman was Daria's twin sister. Boris happened to work with her that morning and became suspicious of her words and actions. Vor detained and questioned her, and it didn't take him long to get a confession from her. She was going to poison you, and she took her own life before we could take it. Daria was found later that day, drugged and locked in a closet."

"And you had no intention of telling me?" Sophia queried loudly to herself more than to Aleksandr. The redhead again tried to push herself off her lover, but he had a vise grip on her legs. "Of course, you didn't. Why would you tell me my life was in danger? Let go of me, Aleksandr! I don't even want to look at you right now. I can't believe someone was here, in this house, ready to kill me, and you didn't tell me!"

"I admit it was a mistake not telling you, Sophia, and I'm sorry for that," Aleksandr replied, the guilt he was feeling intensifying. He had not intended to hurt Sophia or keep the information from her. However, the growing culpability in his chest had Aleksandr reluctantly loosening his grip and allowing her to get up.

"You're only sorry because you had to tell me, dammit," Sophia said, her voice level rising as the rage inside her chest grew. Putting distance between the two of them, she couldn't believe that Aleksandr had hidden the truth from her. "I can't believe I trusted you. You lied to me!"

"I didn't fucking lie to you!" Aleksandr barked back between clenched teeth as he jumped off the couch and stalked toward her. "I was going to tell you about the attempts on your life at some point, but I didn't want to scare you. There was no way in hell that either one of those people were going to get to you, though. I would rather throw myself into a fucking fire than hurt you, baby! I honestly didn't think not telling you would be such a big deal."

"Well, it was. Is there anything else that you haven't told me?" Sophia replied sarcastically, stepping up to him as she put her hands on her hips.

"Don't take that tone with me, pet. I apologized to you. I

suggest you accept it and move on," Aleksandr warned, his tone dark and dangerous as he jerked her closer to him by the front of her shirt.

"I'll do just that," Sophia returned, her own voice icy and void of emotion as Aleksandr let go of her before she turned to head out of the room.

"Where the hell are you going?" Aleksandr questioned, falling in step behind her as she made her way through his home toward the bedroom they shared. He didn't like the tone in Sophia's voice, nor did he like the sudden disconnect he felt from her. When she went to the closet and began pulling out her suitcase, he yelled, "What the fuck are you doing, Sophia? Answer me, dammit!"

Sophia pulled down a pair of jeans before she tossed it in the open suitcase. Looking at Aleksandr, she couldn't stop the tears that began to fall. "You want to go to Vegas and kill Paul, then go, but I won't be here when you get back. With Paul dead, there will be no reason for our little arrangement anymore."

Aleksandr closed his eyes a moment as the vein in his thick neck pulsed. He fought for control of his emotions. Had he heard her right? Did Sophia want to leave him? There was no fucking way he was going to let the little American leave! How could he release the woman he loved? The answer was he couldn't. The bratva leader had honestly thought Sophia was falling in love with him as well, but he must have been wrong. Things had been so damn good between the two of them that he had assumed she felt the same as he. Either way, she was not leaving him. He would do whatever it took to keep her in his home until he returned, even if it meant locking her scrumptious ass up. Opening his eyes as he cracked his neck, Aleksandr said in a deadly calm tone, "You will not leave here, Sophia, until I say you can. Just so you understand my words clearly, I'm not done with you yet, pet, but when I am, you will be the first to know."

"You bastard!" Sophia screamed, throwing the shirt she was holding at him, but he blocked it with his arm. "I should have known I was just sex to you! You can't keep me in this house against my will! I—"

Sophia's words were cut off as Aleksandr swooped in on her like a hawk on its prey. Throwing her over his shoulder, he smacked her soundly on the ass before dumping her on the bed. Before Sophia knew what was happening or could even think of moving off the bed, Aleksandr covered her body with his. However, instead of kissing her, he handcuffed her wrists together and the other end to a metal piece connected with the head of the bed. He then moved off her, but only to remove the jogging pants she wore before flipping her over on the bed. He then brought her up on her knees and began to massage the soft, porcelain cheeks.

"Damn you, Aleksandr! Take these handcuffs off me! If you punish me now, I will hate you!" Sophia shrieked as he tore off the pink bikini underwear she had on. She was already regretting what she said, because she could feel the difference in his touch. Even though she was livid at him, Sophia could not stop her body from responding to Aleksandr. She felt her clit throbbing and the warm, salty liquid running down her inner thighs.

He said nothing in response to her words as his hand came down hard on her bottom. When she cried out, he closed his eyes a moment to keep the tears from falling down his bearded face. The painful sensations in his chest and abdomen were sharp and growing every time he heard Sophia's words replay in his head. He knew she was angry at him and would probably hate him, but there was no way in hell he was going to let her go. Opening his eyes, his hand came down a second time but, this time, on the opposite cheek. He was not surprised to see her stiffen and suddenly grow silent. Damn woman was too fucking stubborn for her own good.

Smacking Sophia's bottom a third, fourth, and fifth time, Aleksandr then bent over and placed a kiss on each flaming red cheek. He let out a loud sigh before he got off the bed. Standing over her, he commanded, "Sophia, look at me." When she turned her head away from him, he could hear her sniffling and knew she was crying. His voice was soft as he said, "I know you are angry at me right now, but because of your attitude and words, you will be kept locked in this bedroom while I'm gone to the States. When I return, we will discuss our relationship, and if at that time you still want to go, I won't stop you. Vor and Boris will look after all your needs while I'm gone."

Aleksandr's heart was breaking as he turned to walk away from her and head toward the door. He fought the urge to turn around and confess his love, but Sophia clearly didn't feel the same. Plus, the redhead's damn stubbornness would keep her from even truly hearing his words. Trying to shake off the soft sobbing he heard coming from the bed, he opened the door of the bedroom and saw Vor standing there. In his native tongue, he said, "You will not be accompanying me to Vegas, Vor. I want you here, watching Sophia."

"Sasha," Vor said in Russian, shaking his head as his eyes locked with Aleksandr's. "I will not allow you to walk into the fucking lion's den without me. If something happened to you—"

"Vor, if something happened to Sophia, I would never forgive myself," Aleksandr replied softly. "With Nikolai and Mikhas in the States, you are the only one I trust to watch over her. She doesn't leave this room until I get back. I don't give a damn what she says. Please, Vor, no arguments on this. You know I'll be safe, and the only way I can do that is if the woman I love is safe as well."

———

Vor glanced over at Sophia, who was still handcuffed on the bed before he looked back at Aleksandr. He had known that Sasha had fallen in love with the American but had hoped he was wrong. Sophia was a good woman whom Vor liked, but the beauty had a bad habit of hurting those closest to her and denying how she felt. Even now, he knew Sophia was scared and didn't want Aleksandr to leave, but instead of saying those words, she was acting like a fucking brat. Vor also could see how tortured Aleksandr was at this moment, and that pissed him off. He had never seen the bratva leader this upset before and hated knowing Sophia was the cause. This was the exact reason why he never planned on falling in love. With an exaggerated exhale, he said, "I'll take good care of Sophia, Sasha, but you do the same. Promise me you will take our most skilled shooters with you, but most of all, come back unharmed. Not only for me but, more importantly, for Sophia."

"Sophia is too angry at me, Vor. I'm not sure she would even care," Aleksandr replied faintly in Russian as he patted his general's face lovingly before he turned and left.

"Aleksandr," Vor heard Sophia say brokenly from the bed in between sobs. "Please be safe. I need you to return to me."

Vor shook his head as he walked over to where the woman was shackled to the bed. Reaching over her, the giant guard unlocked the handcuffs, removed them, and tossed her a robe. He then watched her sit up in the center of the bed and pull on the robe. As she wiped at her eyes and turned her body away from him, he said, "He's gone, Sophia. Your words came too late, I'm afraid."

"Why are you still here, Vor? Shouldn't you be with your precious Sasha?" Sophia asked sarcastically as she turned to look at Vor. Her heart was broken and the last thing she needed was the guard's caustic ridicule of her. The only person that she had ever loved had just walked out on her and she was devastated!

"You fucking little fool! You don't deserve him!" Vor yelled as he hauled her up by her arms. "Why couldn't you just tell him that you love him? Would that have been so hard?"

"Put me down, Vor! Get your hands off me!"

Vor jerked her forward so she could feel his breath on her face. "You can continue to lie to yourself, sweetheart, but I will not allow you to lie to Sasha."

"I didn't lie to Aleksandr about anything!" Sophia screamed back, struggling to break the giant guard's hold. "He's the one who kept the truth from me. He should have told me that someone was here, trying to kill me."

"And if he had? What the fuck do you think you would have done, exactly?" Vor asked in a low, menacing tone. He was seething with rage at the redheaded American. Sophia was hurting Sasha, and he refused to allow that to continue. When Sophia said nothing in response to his question, he scoffed loudly, "Yeah, that's what I thought. You would have done nothing. Like I said, you don't deserve Sasha. You can't even tell him that you want him safe, let alone love him, and here I thought you were courageous. How fucking wrong I was." Vor then released Sophia as she dropped back on the bed and turned to leave the room.

"I fucking love Aleksandr, Vor!" Sophia shrieked as tears once again fell down her face. "He's the one who doesn't give a damn about me. I'm just sex, remember?"

Opening the door to leave, the green-eyed giant turned to

look at Sophia once again. In a restrained, quiet voice he said, "If you were just sex, Sophia, Sasha wouldn't be risking his life to kill the man who wants you dead. If you truly do love him, hopefully you'll get a chance to tell him that." Vor then left the room and slammed the door.

# Chapter 12

The gorgeous, blond Russian walked into the elegant, luxurious Vegas suite and immediately went to the bar. Taking down the bottle of Beluga vodka from the top shelf, Aleksandr tore off the lid and downed half of the clear liquid. As the liquor burned a path down his throat, he slammed the bottle on the bar. He had just killed Morrison and was feeling extremely restless. The fucker had begged for his life, but Aleksandr had cared little. Paul had confessed to killing Viktor and Kira and trying to put Aleksandr behind bars, so he could control the Russian underworld. He had also been the one behind contacting Abrams and entangling Sophia in the mess. However, Paul had insisted that the Chechens, particularly Grecoff, were the masterminds behind the whole plot. Paul had told him that Grecoff not only wanted access to his fortune but his half-sister, Piper Williamson. Apparently, the younger Chechen and Morrison had made a trip to the States once Chechen had found out about the money. They had not only met Piper, but Grecoff had tried to sleep with the woman. Both men had intended on coming back to get the fortune and Piper once Aleksandr and Viktor were out of the picture. Lucky for them, Nikolai had already intercepted the woman and, with her, access to the fortune. Unfortunately, Grecoff had gotten away but had suffered a gunshot wound to the chest. Now all they had to do was find the bastard and end this bullshit. Then maybe Aleksandr could focus on fixing his relationship with Sophia if she wanted one.

Thinking about his beautiful, feisty redhead had a pain shooting across Aleksandr's chest. Grabbing the bottle off the counter, he downed another drink as he walked over to the large, copper-colored sofa and plopped down. Rubbing his tired, silver eyes, he was exhausted and desperately wanted to sleep. However, he had found without Sophia next to him or under him, he couldn't. Aleksandr had been away from her now for almost fifty hours, but it felt like an eternity. He had called to check on her, but she had refused to take his calls. Vor had reported that she had not said a word since Aleksandr left and that worried him. He knew she was angry at him, but had he taken things too far with the punishment? Aleksandr had fought with himself internally and had wanted to scoop her up and make things right before he left the bedroom, but his heart and his pride just wouldn't let him. He had never begged a woman to love him before, and she wouldn't be the first. Even now, as his body ached from the withdrawals of not having Sophia near, Aleksandr would not bow to her. Either Sophia would openly admit to loving him and wanting to stay with him, or he would let her go.

"Hmph! Good luck with that," Aleksandr said to himself before taking another drink of the hard liquor. There was no way in hell he could let Sophia go. The woman had gotten under his skin and he craved her like an addict craving their vice. Aleksandr had often heard Viktor talking about his wife and how she controlled his thoughts and actions even when she wasn't around. He finally understood what the man had meant. He had never expected to find his soulmate, but thanks to that fateful evening in Andrei's club, he had. Now, he just had to find out if she felt the same way he did. Aleksandr understood that Sophia was guarded and always in her head, but he could swear that underneath all of that, she loved him as well. All those nights when they had made love and simply held each other, he had felt so much emotion from her. If he was being truthful with his feelings, he wanted Sophia not only as his lifelong submissive, but also as his wife. He knew he had fucked up, but hopefully his pet could forgive him. Aleksandr would be boarding the plane in an hour, and once he got back to his homeland, he would learn his fate.

Hearing the door to his suite open, Aleksandr watched as his brother, Mikhas, and a stunning blonde with sapphire eyes walked inside. Nikolai had a death grip on the woman's arm, and she looked as though she was ready to beat someone's ass. Walking up to the trio, Aleksandr could see that his brother was seething with a quiet rage of his own. Speaking in Russian, he asked, "Everything okay, Niki?"

"We need to talk privately," Nikolai said between clenched teeth as the woman jerked her arm out of his grip.

"Who's your friend?" Aleksandr asked curiously in English as the blonde's eyes shot to him. The woman was sexy, stacked, beautiful and exactly Nikolai's type. Aleksandr watched intently as his brother leaned over and whispered something in the woman's ear before his hand slid down her back to pat her bottom. Her reaction was to gasp and stiffen immediately. Hiding a chuckle, Aleksandr had never seen his laid back, carefree brother so annoyed. Clearly, his natural good looks and charm weren't working on this woman.

"My name is Piper Williamson, and I can assure you that

Nikolai and I are not friends," the attractive blonde replied sharply as she stepped up to Aleksandr. "Who the hell are you? Do you work for him, like every other man around here does?"

"No, I don't. Nikolai works for me." The slightly taller Volkov smiled as the woman knitted her brow together in confusion. "I'm just kidding, sweetheart. I'm Nikolai's older, more attractive brother Aleksandr. It's nice to finally meet you, Piper. Sorry we had to meet under circumstances such as these. I will admit that you are not what I was expecting."

"Don't expect anything from her, brother. This one belongs to me," Nikolai warned in Russian as he slid his arm protectively around her waist. Then to the voluptuous blonde, Nikolai said, "I need to talk to my brother, Piper. Wait in the bedroom for me. I'll join you shortly. We can talk then about what occurred tonight."

Piper nodded her head before Nikolai kissed her softly on the neck. Aleksandr could tell the woman was internally seething and wanted to verbally lash out, but instead, she walked away.

When the older Volkov heard the bedroom door close, he gave his brother the bottle of vodka. As Nikolai took a long swallow, Aleksandr said, "You looked like you could use a drink. Feeling a little tense this evening?"

"You don't know the half of it," Nikolai responded, taking another long swig of the vodka.

"Looks like Ms. Williamson is quite the handful," Aleksandr said, taking a seat on the sofa before he propped his feet up on the glass coffee table. "I take it the two of you don't get along very well?"

Nikolai didn't appreciate the smile he saw on his brother's face or the teasing nature of his tone. His mood was actually quite dark. "I'm not in the mood to talk about my interactions with Piper tonight, Zan. We have other problems."

"Such as?"

"One of our men saw Grecoff get picked up in a white van near the warehouse. We found a damaged bulletproof vest at the pickup spot. I guarantee it was his, so that means the fucker isn't dead. Were you able to get any more information from Paul?"

"Morrison was insistent that the Chechens were behind the whole plan. Honestly, I'm not surprised. I made sure to record the confession so the council can see it. He also said that he and Grecoff had met with Piper about a month and a half ago. Has she mentioned that to you?"

"She did. Piper told me she was approached by them one night and that Grecoff wanted sex. She told him no and he hit her a couple of times, but she was able to get out of there without anything else happening. Piper also said Paul never mentioned anything about being her half-brother or the money. She only discovered that piece of information after we met."

"Do you believe Piper? What's her story?" Aleksandr asked, watching his brother's eyes as they kept averting to the hallway that led to the bedroom where Piper was.

"I do. Everything she's told me so far has checked out," Nikolai responded before dropping down in the chair perpendicular to his brother. "As for Piper, she's a medical student who works part time in a sex club as a dominatrix. She's twenty-three and has had a pretty rough past, based on what we have found. She hasn't confirmed a lot of the history because she's reluctant to talk about it."

Aleksandr rubbed his bearded chin as he listened to Nikolai speak. Sounded like he needed to investigate Ms. Williamson's past himself. His brother was clearly interested in the blonde beauty and there was no way in hell Aleksandr would let anyone hurt Nikolai. "We know Paul is corrupt and has been for several years. Is Piper?"

"No," the younger Volkov said, shaking his head before he took another drink. "If she's anything, it's too honest. She's quite the enigma, reminds me of Sophia to some degree. Piper is emotionally damaged like your American and won't allow herself to be happy."

"Tell me about it," Aleksandr scoffed, rolling his eyes before running an agitated hand through his dirty-blond hair. Looking directly into eyes the same as his, he asked, "Have you slept with Piper? I want the truth, Niki."

It was moments like this that Nikolai hated his bond with his brother. Aleksandr had always been able to read him like an open book, without Nikolai saying a word. Without batting an eye, he said, "Yes, I have. Several times, in fact, and I plan on doing it again. I'm going to bring Piper back to Russia with me until I can kill Grecoff. Do you have any problems with that?"

"Should I?"

"No."

"Good, because I got my own shit to worry about right now," Aleksandr countered, taking the bottle of vodka from his brother and taking another drink. "You know the council is pushing for me to take over. If I do it, I want you right there beside me. How would you feel about that?"

"You know I would have no problems with it, Zan, so why don't you tell me what is really on your mind?" Nikolai replied worriedly as he watched his brother's gaze go to the wall that was one large window. Outside, the Vegas lights twinkled below them. "You've been in a shitty mood since your plane landed. Plus, don't think I haven't noticed that Vor isn't here. I'm assuming something has happened between you and Sophia. Care to talk about it?"

"Yeah, I do." Aleksandr sighed, keeping his eyes on the city lights outside. The bratva leader really didn't want to involve his younger brother in his relationship problems when he was clearly having issues of his own.

"Come on, Zan. I know you see me as your little brother, but I'm a grown man. I also happen to like Sophia. We've dealt with shit like Morrison and Chechen our whole fucking lives and you've never shown emotion like this. That only leaves one person as the source of your foul mood."

Finally looking at Nikolai, Aleksandr's voice was soft and full of emotion as he said, "I fucked things up with Sophia and I don't know how to fix it."

"I doubt that. What happened?" the younger Volkov asked. He had never in his life seen his older brother emotional over anything, let alone a woman.

"Sophia thinks I lied to her," Aleksandr scoffed, running an agitated hand through his hair as he removed his feet from the coffee table and leaned forward by placing his elbows on his knees. "She's out of her fucking mind because I've never lied to anyone in my life. So, I didn't tell her about the attempts on her life while she was in my home. That's not me lying about the shit. I just didn't fucking tell her. I wanted her to feel safe in my home. I wanted her to enjoy being there with me. I wanted... I wanted her to fall in love with me, Nik."

Reaching out, Nikolai affectionately rubbed his brother's broad shoulder. "I think she has, Zan," Nikolai said as his brother's eyes met his. "You don't know this, but I was hoping to share Sophia with you and made the mistake of expressing that to her. She let me know quickly that she belonged to you and you alone. I see the way she looks at you. She loves you, too; she's just scared to admit it. Given her past, I can understand why."

Aleksandr leaned back and spread his arms out on the couch. He closed his eyes a minute as he let Nikolai's words sink in. Sophia had told him all about her family and how she felt responsible for their deaths. He also understood how his life mirrored her father's, whom Sophia had been extremely close to. Aleksandr saw firsthand how his woman struggled with expressing her feelings verbally. Sophia was quirky and often tried hiding her feelings from him, but when they made love, those were the times she was authentic with her emotions. The Russian billionaire felt deeply connected to his submissive, but just when he felt the closest to her, Sophia pulled away. Maybe that was her coping mechanism for when things got too hard, and if it was, how did he break that cycle? Aleksandr loved Sophia and wanted her to feel the same but not if it felt forced.

"Are you willing to fight for Sophia, Zan?" Nikolai questioned as his brother's silver eyes immediately shot to his. "If you are, then go get your damn woman, but if you're not, let her go. Sophia is a risk worth taking and I've never known you to walk away from a challenge."

Before Aleksandr could respond to his brother, Mikhas walked into the room. Looking directly at the elder Volkov, he said, "I'm sorry to interrupt, boss, but the pilot called and the plane is ready."

"Thank you, Mikhas. Call Petya and have him meet me downstairs with the car in five." When his second in command walked away, Aleksandr stood up and grabbed his jacket off the back of the nearby chair. Looking at Nikolai, a smile touched his face. "Thanks for the pep talk, Niki, and by the way, Sophia is worth it. Will I see you back in Russia soon?"

Nikolai stood up and pulled his brother in for a tight, loving embrace. Pulling back, he grabbed Aleksandr by the nape of his neck. "Da. Give me a day or two to finish up here and I'll be home. Go easy on Sophia, okay? It will all work out in the end."

"Of course, it will. I'm one hell of a catch." Aleksandr smiled before he patted Nikolai's face lovingly and headed toward the door.

Across the world, outside of Moscow, Vor walked up the stairs and down the long hall toward the bedroom. Once he reached the door of the room, he knocked. When he heard the soft voice on the other side telling him to enter, he did just that. His green eyes immediately found the magenta-haired beauty sitting in the center of the bed, reading a book. She was dressed in dark grey yoga pants and a black, long-sleeved Henley shirt. There was also a full tray of food sitting beside her on the bed. That was the reason he was checking on Sophia. Boris had reported to him that the woman was not eating, and he didn't want her starving herself, especially because that would anger Aleksandr. Plus, despite his past interactions with her, Vor did like the American.

"What do you want, Vor?" Sophia asked, turning the page of her book without looking up at him. Even though she held the book in her hands, she couldn't focus on it. She had been ridiculously miserable without Aleksandr, and what made things worse was that she was trapped in a room that smelled just like him.

"Boris reported that you haven't been eating," Vor replied, taking a seat on the edge of the bed.

Sophia laughed caustically as she rolled her eyes. "Really? That's why you're visiting me? You suddenly care about what I eat?"

"I care because Sasha does," Vor said softly, carefully watching her demeanor. "Answer me honestly, Sophia. Are you not feeling well?"

"I just don't feel like eating." Sophia sighed honestly as she put away the book and crossed her legs in the center of the bed. When her eyes connected with Vor's, she said, "Look, I'm not sick or coming down with anything. I just miss Aleksandr terribly and this horrible, nauseating feeling of guilt is just sitting in my stomach like a rock."

Vor was astonished to hear the American openly admit her feelings to him. Sophia had not said three words to him in the last two days, but here she was, admitting her deepest emotions. The woman confused the hell out of him, so he couldn't even begin to understand how Sasha felt dealing with her. The woman was quite the conundrum! Sensing her vulnerability, Vor replied gently, "So, you made a mistake. You don't need to beat yourself up over this. The solution is simple little one, and I think you know what you need to do."

"But what if he doesn't accept my apology?" Sophia questioned, unshed tears in her eyes. She had replayed the whole conversation with Aleksandr a million times in her head. The redhead had already determined that there was no way she would recover if she lost him, but that didn't give her the right to be so cruel to him verbally. Her words, unfortunately, had stemmed from this overwhelming fear. What if she had damaged their relationship beyond repair? Her lover had been so angry at her, and she hated the pain she'd seen deep in his eyes.

"I've never known Sasha to hold a grudge," Vor answered honestly. "I think if you're sincere about the apology, it will show. I can't speak for him, but I think things between the two of you will be fine."

"You've heard from him, right? Aleksandr's okay?"

"I have, and he is. He is on his way home, actually. The plane just left Vegas."

Sophia closed her eyes a moment as she thanked her creator for keeping Aleksandr safe and unharmed. Feeling the tears on her cheek, she wiped them away. Looking at Vor again, she asked, "Are Paul and Grecoff dead?"

"Paul is, but Grecoff is not. I'm not sure what all Sasha wants you to know, so I will let him elaborate on the latter part of that," Vor replied as he watched Sophia intently. She was so difficult to read at times, but the guard really wanted to understand what the woman was feeling. "Let's say that all is forgiven when Sasha comes home and you two maintain a relationship. Are you going to be able to handle his lifestyle? Word of advice, you either need to accept it or move on, Sophia. He was born into this life and I can't see him leaving it. I know your relationship with him is new, but you must learn to trust him. You can't continue to fight him on every single decision he makes. I've known Sasha most of my life, and when it comes to the bratva, the safety of his friends and family are his first priority. He will never, and let me stress never, put those he cares for in harm's way. Despite the role he leads, Sasha is a man of integrity, honesty, and character. Think you can handle that?"

"I want to. I really do," Sophia responded softly as she wrung the hands in her lap nervously. "I understand the bratva is important to Aleksandr, but it's dangerous and I hate the thought of him being vulnerable. He may keep those he cares for safe, but what about himself, Vor? Aleksandr is not invincible, although he thinks he is. You and I both know you can't always be there to protect him, and shit doesn't always go as planned. Don't you worry about him?"

"All the time, Sophia, but I trust Sasha completely," Vor said, a small smile tugging at the corners of his mouth. "And the only way it is going to work between the two of you is if you do the same. You're just going to have to figure out whether or not you want to take such a large leap of faith. You said you loved Sasha. If that's true, then you will ultimately do what's right."

"And if I can't, then what?" Sophia asked, whisper soft, unable to look at Vor.

"Then you'll lose him," Vor responded with an equally quiet voice as Sophia buried her face in her hands. Letting out a deep breath, he stood and walked toward the door of the bedroom. Opening the door, he said over his shoulder, "I hope you make the right decision, but it's yours to make. Personally, if I loved someone like you say you do, a few minutes of happiness are a hell of a lot better than none at all."

Sophia let out a loud scream of frustration as she picked up the book and threw it toward the door Vor had just closed. Could she let go of her greatest fear and give herself completely to Aleksandr? Every fiber of her being told her to, but could she be that vulnerable to someone? She knew Aleksandr was not her father, but that didn't make accepting his lifestyle any easier. Being the leader of the Russian underworld, meant that her lover would always be in danger. Could she live her life like that daily? What if the relationship went even further and they had children? Shaking her head fiercely, Sophia jumped off the bed and walked over to the window that encompassed one whole wall of Aleksandr's bedroom. There was no way in hell she could live like that.

Pressing her forehead against the cool, tempered glass, Sophia looked at the beautiful countryside. Tears streamed down her face as she thought about a life without Aleksandr. What the hell was she going to do? Vor was right; she would rather have Aleksandr in her life for a short time than not at all. She didn't know how it had happened, but she loved him. What had started as pure sex, had evolved into an all-encompassing love and passion for the man. Sophia's gorgeous lover had accepted her vulnerability and what she considered her difficult personality without batting an eye. Not once had her Russian abused his power over her. Aleksandr had done quite the opposite, really, by treating her with a genuine love and compassion. She loved their conversations and the ease in which they just jibed with one another. Sophia also found herself enjoying Aleksandr's homeland and her time working with Artem. Would it be so bad to live with her blond dominant in his home and finally allow herself love? The answer was no. How could having everything she wanted be bad?

*What the hell am I going to do?* Sophia thought to herself. Vor was right. The choice was hers, but could she make the right decision?

# Chapter 13

Sophia sat in the window seat of Aleksandr's private library as she watched the icy rain begin to fall outside. The afternoon sky was just beginning to darken, and a tumultuous snowstorm was headed their way. Hugging her legs closer to her body, she was a bundle of nerves and fear. The beautiful redhead had no idea what she was going to say to Aleksandr, but she did know that she wanted, no needed, the Russian in her life. *Pride be damned,* Sophia said to herself. She was miserable without Aleksandr and the guilt was eating her alive inside. When Vor had announced that her lover would be home soon, she had found herself almost running downstairs to greet him. She had been ready almost an hour ago to confess her undying love to Aleksandr, but now that she had time to think about it, Sophia wasn't so sure. *No, you love him,* she argued with herself, *and you will tell him.* Aleksandr would either push her out the door or pull her close to him and profess his love back. Sophia had prayed to her creator that it would be the latter. She was tired of being alone, and Aleksandr had not only shown her how much she needed him in her life, but he had also taught her that there was more to life than just work.

After speaking to Vor, Sophia had given the whole relationship with Aleksandr thought. She still wasn't sure how it had happened, but there was no denying that she had fallen in love with her dominant. The sexual chemistry between the two of them was all-consuming but went so much deeper than that. Sophia felt safe and loved with Aleksandr, and those were two feelings that had been missing from her life for a long time. Even now, her body physically ached for him. Since her Russian left, she had been joyless and despondent, especially knowing she had hurt Aleksandr the way she had. Although she had initially seen the changes in her life as horribly drastic, she now saw them as a type of blessing. Aleksandr had taken her out of the austere, monotonous world she had been living in and thrust her into a new and exciting realm that felt like an erotic fairy tale. Sophia only hoped that her fairy tale would have a happy ending. She prayed that Vor was right and Aleksandr would forgive her, but she still ran the risk of him not loving her. Even if the blond billionaire didn't, maybe over time, she could change his mind. After all, Vor had told her to take a giant leap of faith, and that was exactly what she was going to do, even if it meant falling flat on her face.

Seeing the bright headlights cutting through the rain as they rounded the curve of the drive, Sophia felt her heart begin to pound in her chest. Jumping off the window seat, she quickly ran toward the front door of Aleksandr's home. Flinging open the door, she was unprepared for the icy cold wind that cut through her slender frame. Wrapping her arms around herself tightly, she watched as Aleksandr's car pulled up to the front of the house. When he stepped out of the car, Sophia took off running through the torrential, frigid rain and threw herself in his arms. Her lips devoured his and her legs wrapped around his waist as he fell back against the car with his arms locked around her.

"I'm so sorry, Aleksandr!" Sophia said breathlessly between sloppy kisses. "Please forgive me. I never meant to hurt you, baby. I'm so sorry."

---

Aleksandr steadied himself against the car as his hands roamed her body and he took over the kiss. Had he just heard Sophia apologize? He had already decided on the plane ride home that he was going to make Sophia love him, one way or another. He had absolutely no intention of letting her go, but his magenta-haired American had managed to surprise him once again. He had not expected her apology, but he sure the fuck would take it.

Breaking the kiss, Sophia hugged Aleksandr to her chest as she shivered uncontrollably. Her blond lover had not responded to her yet. Was he still angry at her? Maybe he had not heard her over the thunderous downpour. The rain hid the tears falling down her face as she looked into his eyes and rambled loudly, "Please don't be angry at me, baby. I'm so sorry about the way I treated you. I was just so scared I was going to lose you when you left. If something happened to you, I would just die. I was being stupid. Can you please forgive me? I'll do anything I can to make it up to you. I love you so damn much! I—"

"What did you just fucking say to me?" Aleksandr asked, astonishment written all over his wet face as he gripped her lovely, porcelain face in his hands. A smile touched his hand-some, bearded face before he kissed her soundly on her blue, shivering lips once more. "Say it again, Sophia. What did you just say?"

"I said I love you. I..." Sophia replied softly, but before she

185

could say anything else, she was thrown over Aleksandr's shoulder as he sprinted into the house. She felt so conflicted and couldn't tell if her lover had been happy or upset with her words. All she knew was that he had not said it back. Sophia couldn't help but feel the painful lump forming in her chest. What the hell could she do to make this man love her as she loved him?

Walking into the large, luxurious bathroom, Aleksandr could barely contain his happiness. His beautiful submissive had not only told him once that she loved him but twice. He could not even begin to express the sheer joy swelling within him or the sudden need to possess every single inch of his Sophia. As he put the petite redhead on her feet, he began removing his own wet clothes as he barked, "Take off your clothes, and do it now!"

---

Sophia watched in silence as Aleksandr momentarily disappeared into the oversized, modern, rain sky shower before he came back after removing his clothes. She watched the steam from the multiple shower heads caress his tattooed skin only seconds before she, too, began to remove the soaking wet material from her body. She felt the heat flood her body and her core moisten as the dominant's silver eyes devoured her. Aleksandr had not said he loved her, but he clearly still wanted her sexually. She gasped loudly when a very naked Aleksandr roughly pulled her into his arms and jerked the rest of her clothes off. She sighed into his mouth when it hungrily found hers before he picked her up under her legs and carried her into the shower.

He pulled them under the hot, steamy water as his tongue mated with hers. His engorged, massive cock rubbing against her wet pussy lips as her arms pulled at his blond hair. Pushing her back against the glass, Aleksandr eased the head of his dick into her dripping wet core but went no farther. He then trailed across her shoulder and neck. Again, she saw that he could not stop the boyish grin from forming on his lips.

"Aleksandr," Sophia softly whispered as his eyes met hers. She nervously nibbled on her lip as she continued, "Are you still angry at me? You haven't really said anything to me. I know I messed up—"

"Shh, pet," her blond dominant responded as he buried himself balls deep inside her. As they both moaned in luxurious passion, he brushed her wet hair back from her face and lightly kissed her lips. Gazing deep into her eyes, he smiled. "I need you to stop worrying. I'm not mad at you, sweetheart. I actually love you as much as you love me."

Sophia stared at Aleksandr a moment before his words perforated her confused mind. The smile that lit her face, though, when they did was positively breathtaking. She smashed her lips to his in a hard, passionate kiss before she broke the kiss and began to laugh. "You mean it, baby?" she asked, tears of joy brimming in her eyes. "You really love me because I love you so much? I don't know why I didn't tell you that before you left, but I guess I wasn't ready. I'm not sure how we are going to make this work but—"

Aleksandr silenced her words with another kiss as he began to move his cock slowly in and out of her tight pussy.

Her eyes glazed back over with passion as he chuckled deeply. Sophia fell into a rhythm with him by undulating her hips against his and kneading the muscles on his chest.

Pulling at her earlobe with his teeth, he huskily whispered, "I thought that might shut you up. We'll make this work, baby. Besides, we have the rest of our lives to figure it out."

"I know we do." Sophia giggled, hugging Aleksandr to her chest. She purred, "Make love to me, Sir. Fuck my pussy hard."

An animalistic growl escaped Aleksandr's mouth before he gripped her thighs and began to pound himself inside her at a maddening pace. He moaned when her small hands pulled painfully at his hair as she rode his cock with equal force as his thrusts. His dick throbbed with a greater intensity when her porcelain breasts created friction on his chest as they bounced up and down with each undulation of his hips. Feeling his own, and Sophia's sweet body, on the edge of an incredible climax, the Russian billionaire stopped his movements and gripped her throat loosely with one large hand.

"No, dammit!" Sophia pleaded, reaching between their bodies to fondle his balls. "Don't stop! I was almost there!"

"What did you say, pet?" he asked heatedly, his tongue running across her lips. "That wasn't an order I heard escape that luscious mouth, was it? Have you already forgotten your place?"

"No, Sir, I haven't," Sophia replied, swallowing the lump in her throat. She loved it when Aleksandr played dirty. "I just missed having you inside me. What is it that you want from me, Sir?"

A shiver ran through Aleksandr's large body as he raised Sophia up and off his hard cock and put her back on her feet. He then turned her around and brushed her hair from her neck as his mouth blazed a trail along the delicate skin. As he feasted on her shoulder, he spread her ass cheeks apart and placed his massive, erect dick in between them. He then slapped her bottom and chuckled when she, again, purred and rubbed against him like a well-fed cat. "I want to slip inside here, pet," Aleksandr said in a deep, savage voice. "Will you let me?"

Sophia hesitated a moment as she anxiously chewed on her bottom lip. She had enjoyed the anal play and wanted to please Aleksandr, but she was scared. Her magenta head fell back against his chest when his thick digits began to pluck and massage her clit. "Oh, I want to so bad, Sir." Sophia began loving the way his free hand roamed her breasts. "Can you promise me I'll like it?"

"I promise." Aleksandr grinned, wanting to ease her fears. "It will feel unlike anything you have felt before. If you get uncomfortable, you know the drill."

The giant billionaire then smacked her ass once more before he pulled away momentarily to get out of the shower and grab some lubricant. Pouring a small amount in his hand, he rubbed his cock slowly as he walked back over to her. He captured her lips and mouthed 'I love you' before he turned her around and spread her bottom. His free hand slid back into her warm pussy and, once again, began to manipulate her clit. Then he positioned the head of his cock at her anal opening. Next to her ear, he breathed, "Relax, pet. This is going to feel uncomfortable at first, but I need you to trust me."

"I do. I love you," Sophia mumbled breathlessly, his fingers driving her closer and closer to an orgasm. She then gasped loudly in pain and discomfort when Aleksandr eased himself into the opening until he was fully embedded in her bottom. Sophia told herself to relax and focus on the pleasure his fingers were causing. The discomfort melted quickly as the orgasm ripped through her petite frame and flooded into his hand and down her inner thighs. Her vaginal walls quivered and convulsed as he began to move his cock in and out of her ass. As he pushed himself back in, Sophia felt his balls slap against her pussy. Just as the sensations began to subside from the first release, he began working her into a second, more powerful one.

Sweat poured off Aleksandr's chest as he pumped himself inside Sophia's delicious bottom, the satisfaction he was receiving from the tight, virgin warmth magnificent and beyond words. His little wanton submissive was adding to his rapture by assisting his movements as she squirmed in delight on his fingers. He felt his balls begin to tighten and the pressure of his own climax building as he fucked her harder, deeper, and faster. When the second orgasm tore through Sophia's body, he grabbed her hips tightly and buried his cock as deep as he could inside her bottom. At that moment, he released his hot liquid love inside her warmth as he yelled out and gripped her hips. His massive, muscular frame bucked and jerked against hers before he turned her face and captured her lips in a hot, passionate kiss. Aleksandr then slipped himself from her warmth and turned her around in his arms. The two of them simply held each other and kissed as the pulsing water poured down over them.

After a few minutes of simply loving one another under the warm, clear water, Sophia pulled away from Aleksandr's arms. Before she could get far, he jerked her back into his arms. "Don't worry, baby." She smiled, kissing his lips and loving his possessive nature. "I was just going to grab the soap and bathe my man."

Cupping her face in both of his hands, he searched her eyes as he said, "I think that sounds wonderful. I just wanted to make sure you weren't overthinking what just transpired between the two of us and running away."

Placing a butterfly kiss on his lips, Sophia grinned. "Nope. I still love you. Just thought I could take care of my man, especially since I was so horrible to him before he left."

"I'm sorry, too, Sophia. I never should have punished you like that and then left. I just felt so—"

"Rejected? Yeah, I know," Sophia said gently, finishing his thought. "I saw the pain flash in your eyes, and that hurt me more than anything. I was just being stupid when I let you leave."

"Not stupid, emotional. Big difference." Aleksandr half

smiled before he smacked her soundly on the ass. "Now pamper your man, woman."

Sophia giggled before she grabbed the soap. When she came back to her lover, the redhead ran her finger along his semi-hard cock before gliding it up his abdomen and chest.

Her giant lover let out a growl and pushed her hand away as he lifted a golden brow.

"I'll be good, baby. I just couldn't help myself." Sophia smiled seductively as she poured the masculine smelling soap in her hands and began massaging Aleksandr's upper body. As she did this, she said, "So I guess we need to talk."

"About?"

"Us," Sophia answered gently, loving the feel of his hard, muscular body under her small hands. "Since Paul is dead, there is really no reason for us to continue our initial deal. However, since we have gone and fallen in love with one another, where do we go from here? Have you given it any thought?"

"No need to, sweetness," Aleksandr casually countered as he enjoyed the feel of her hands on his body. He could already feel his cock responding to her touch and the proximity of her presence. "You will continue to live with me just as you are now. I would like to continue our Dominant/submissive relationship but move this into a long-term thing, maybe even marriage, down the road. Even if you hadn't professed your love, you weren't going anywhere."

"Marriage? Whoa, partner… one step at a time." Sophia chuckled nervously, although the thought of marrying Aleksandr had the most wonderful sensation forming in the pit of her stomach. "I will admit, though, it makes me happy to hear that you weren't going to let me leave. Even though you couldn't tell, I have loved you for a while now. What about you?"

Aleksandr hugged Sophia to him tightly as he placed kisses

along her jawline. Pulling back to look into her eyes, he said, "Since the first night I saw you in the club, I knew there was something different about you from the start. You're the first woman I have ever had that reaction to, sweetheart."

"Same here," she softly answered, giving him more room to her neck and shoulders. As his fingers playfully plucked at her nipples, Sophia felt the wetness forming between her legs again. Forcing herself to concentrate on anything but the pleasure, she said, "Stop trying to distract me, dammit! We are talking, remember?"

"Oh, that's right." Aleksandr seductively grinned, feeling the pulse in her slender neck quicken with arousal. He loved that she was so open with her emotions and humoring her for a moment longer, he said, "Artem told me that you have been advising him on a handful of cases. Is there a collaboration in the future?"

"Yes. Artem is a great guy and a brilliant lawyer. I'm looking forward to working with him. I do get to leave the house to work, right?"

"You do, however, you will have guards with you at all times. That is not negotiable," he said sternly as his hand patted her round bottom.

"Yeah, this dominance thing you do. I'm okay with continuing it in the bedroom, but I would like for us to move into more of an equal partnership outside of it. How would you feel about that?"

"It'll be hard for me, but I can work on that." Aleksandr sighed as Sophia's soapy hands found his cock and began to massage it. "Don't expect change overnight, though, pet."

Sophia responded by placing kisses on his chest before she rubbed her face against the light blond hair there. She couldn't help the stunning smile that played on her lips. Her lover was willing to meet her halfway, well kind of. As she fondled him in long, deliberate strokes, Sophia felt Aleksandr's hand slide down her stomach toward her core. Before his fingers slid between the silky folds, the redhead grabbed his hand and looped it in hers as she hungrily whispered, "No, Aleksandr. Let me please you first."

"And what exactly did you have in mind, pet?" he asked, kissing the back of the hand he held. He couldn't help the precum that oozed from the head of his cock at Sophia's gentle fondling. The Russian's silver eyes darkened with lust when he watched her lick his seed from her finger. The growl caught in his throat when Sophia stared into his eyes intently while she lowered herself before him. His blond head fell back in ecstasy when her tongue ran across the slit of his throbbing manhood. When her hot, sweet mouth swallowed him whole, Aleksandr gripped her magenta hair in his fist as his stomach muscles uncontrollably flexed. Fuck, this woman would be the death of him!

Releasing his cock with a pop, Sophia licked her lips ravenously as she smiled up at him. She saw the raw, unadulterated lust in his eyes. She absolutely loved the effect she had on her lover. "Mmm, so yummy," she teased, lovingly rubbing the hardened skin against her face. "May I have another taste, Master?"

Aleksandr couldn't help the shiver that tore through his body as he watched his submissive. "Yes, pet. Take it deep into your mouth this time," he hoarsely replied, strengthening his hold on her hair before directing his cock back into her mouth. He could feel his balls again tighten as Sophia relaxed her neck muscles and deep throated him. His sweat mixed with the water pouring down over them when he began to fuck her lovely mouth slowly. When she began to massage his scrotum and ass as she sucked him deeper and deeper in her throat, Aleksandr pulled out of her mouth quickly before he exploded. Jerking her up roughly, his mouth devoured hers. "Such a dirty little fucking submissive!" he snarled breathlessly against her lips. "You were trying to make me come, weren't you?"

"Yes, Sir," Sophia admitted, rubbing her face against his. Her own clit throbbed painfully as the wetness dripped from her core. "Don't you want to come in my mouth, Master?"

"No," Aleksandr replied huskily as her eyes flew to his. "I want to come in that sweet, tight pussy."

Sophia cried out in girlish delight when Aleksandr picked her up and carried her to the large bed, still wet from the shower. As he tossed her on the soft, plush mattress, she barely had time to think before her legs were spread wide and he was there. Her petite hands gripped his blond hair, and she smashed her lips against his as he eased his cock into her vaginal opening. However, before she could deepen the kiss, Aleksandr had her hands locked above her head and began to roughly pump himself in and out of her tight cunt. Sophia panted and squirmed underneath him as she cried out in euphoria from his thrusts. When his hot mouth found one, pert nipple, she screamed as the orgasm unexpectedly tore through her body.

At the moment of Sophia's release, Aleksandr released her hands and buried his cock balls deep inside of her. He stilled his movements and watched in wonder as his beautiful submissive convulsed and shook in blissful pleasure. He loved the way Sophia's heels dug into his ass and she buried her face against his thick, corded neck as she rode the wave of her orgasm. Before she could even begin to relax, he flipped her over on her stomach, grabbed her hips, and pulled her back against his groin. He then smacked her soundly on her bottom before he plunged back inside her tight, wet core. Reaching under her petite frame, he gripped her breasts in his large hands and slammed her back against his chest. Needing to find his own release, Aleksandr pounded Sophia's pussy wildly as the two of them panted breathlessly and sweat dripped from his darkened skin. Feeling his balls constrict, Aleksandr bit down on her slender shoulder as his own orgasm shot from his cock. As the semen poured from him, he felt a second wave of pleasure pulse through Sophia. Her vaginal walls contracting only added to the intensity of his own release. With a final grunt of satisfaction, the blond giant collapsed on top of Sophia.

Sophia's breathing returned to normal as Aleksandr rubbed his bearded face against her shoulder and neck before he placed kisses across her face. She loved the way his hands roamed her diminutive form and the way his body eclipsed hers. *And to think, you almost gave all of this up*, Sophia scolded herself as she snuggled the pillow beneath her. Closing her eyes, she just allowed herself to become one with her lover. Before drifting off to sleep, she felt Aleksandr move off her long enough to pull the covers up over them and then settle back against her. "Do you still love me, Aleksandr?"

"Always, Sophia." Aleksandr smiled before he, too, fell asleep. "Always."

The End

## Jessie Jones

My name is Jessie Jones and I am a 43-year-old woman who is a new author with Blushing Books Publications. My debut novel, "The Taking," is the first installment of the "Finding Forever" series. I have been telling stories since I was old enough to talk, however, didn't begin writing them down until I was about 7 years old. I am currently not married, and I live in the Middle of Nowhere Indiana with my sister, nephew, and 5 rescue babies (all dogs). When I am not writing steamy, erotic romances you will find me traveling, ghost hunting, watching scary movies, playing with the four-legged babies, and listening to Panic at the Disco.

You can connect with me on Facebook at https://www. facebook.com/profile.php?id=100045892626808 or at Twitter at https://twitter.com/JessieJBooks . You can also email me directly at jessiejonesromance2019@gmail.com

Don't miss these exciting titles by Jessie Jones and Blushing Books!

*Finding Forever Series*
The Taking
The Seduction
The Falling
The Coming Storm
The Road to Redemption
Endless Love

*His Reluctant Submissive Series*
Aleksandr

## Blushing Books

Blushing Books is one of the oldest eBook publishers on the web. We've been running websites that publish spanking and BDSM related romance and erotica since 1999, and we have been selling eBooks since 2003. We hope you'll check out our hundreds of offerings at http://www.blushingbooks.com.

## Blushing Books Newsletter

Please join the Blushing Books newsletter
to receive updates & special promotional offers.
You can also join by using your mobile phone:
Just text BLUSHING to 22828.